Reclamation

Jon Christian

Literary Wanderlust | Denver, Colorado

Published in the United States by Literary Wanderlust LLC, Denver, Colorado.
https//www.LiteraryWanderlust.com

ISBN Print: 978-1-942856-66-5
ISBN Digital: 978-1-942856-69-6

Cover design: Pozo Mitsuma

Printed in the United States of America

Dedication

For Dustin and Ryder

To seek is to find
To find is to understand
To understand is to love
And to love is to commit.

Acknowledgments

I would like to thank Suzie Brooks for challenging me to the max, and always being able to smell the granola through the tin foil. Krissy Singleton for believing in me and embracing my oddity. Sarah Doze for her sage advice and patient heart. Kim Rutigliano for getting things ready, and Kleaver for always feeling the groove.

1

Case didn't want to be governed. His pursuit of emancipation was fraught with defection, but he didn't think it would end within the boundaries he established. He took a glass of water from Reed and drank ferociously. "I don't know why you are holding me here. I'm not a threat to you or anyone," Case said, trying to sound diplomatic. "I'm on my way to the United States to stop them from killing the people in Eads."

He glanced around his interrogation cell. Though he hadn't seen working electricity in four years, fluorescent bulbs filled this sterile room with blinding light. The walls and floor were as white as virgin bed sheets. The obscene brightness made Case disoriented. Case's legs shook, and he opened and closed his fists as he tried to regain control of his emotions. In a peculiar way, the lit room reminded Case of dim times. A time of a Second Civil War, where battles for access to natural resources ruled; secession tore the United States into three distinct, yet separate territories—the United States, and the Texas and Colorado territories.

"Mr. Tappan," Reed, a devout engineer and scientist, said, "This is Project Grid." He opened his arms wide, a gesture of proud yet protective ownership. Reed may as well have been introducing his children. "We are devoted to the continued freedom of the Colorado Territory. As you have noticed, this location has working electricity. Above ground are hundreds of towering windmills, and I am only a year away from bringing wind power to everyone within our boundaries."

Less than an hour ago, Reed had abruptly removed Case from his diplomatic mission to the state of Kansas, now the eastern border of the Colorado Territory and the US. Case had been escorted down a set of stairs, through a long hall and directly into this room. He was underneath the windmills he noticed on his trip. At the time, he assumed they were abandoned units, much like any source of power in the ten former states.

"I have squeezed blood from my soul to make this a reality," Reed continued. "I have hardly slept to make this happen. I've spent those sleepless nights reviewing schematics by candlelight. And now you've come along to disrupt all of this? I don't think so."

Reed's husky voice was practiced and patient as if he'd rehearsed this conversation before. With his razor-cut short hair, he looked to be in his mid-twenties, not much older than Case. He wore a plain white T-shirt and jeans, torn from work, not for fashion. His intense brown eyes shifted rapidly. He processed information like a computer. Everything Reed planned, he expected a return on his investment.

Case leaned back against a white, unforgiving metal chair. His water glass glistened in the bright light atop a bone-white folding table. It was the kind of table Case would have used for a backyard picnic. Only this wasn't a backyard picnic.

"I only want a peaceful resolution," Case said. "I don't want to disrupt what you've done."

"Who do you plan to speak with, Mr. Tappan? What exactly is your objective when you get to Kansas?" Reed asked.

"I will request to speak with US officials," Case said. "My objective will be a new treaty that establishes peace between the United States and the Colorado Territory. One that President Everett will sign."

"Who gives you the authority?" Reed asked.

"You know it was me who signed the secession treaty," Case said. "I am the most logical person to negotiate peace. After all, no one in the Colorado Territory was killed during the Second Civil War, and no one has to die today, either."

The past four years post-secession had brought many struggles, and all along Case kept to his main objective—peace through diplomacy. Despite the civil war between the Texas Territory and the United States, not one bullet flew in the former states of Colorado, Utah, New Mexico, Nevada, Wyoming, Montana, Oklahoma, Idaho, North and South Dakota—collectively referred to as the Colorado Territory. Case's diplomacy resulted in independence for the territory written into a treaty, signed by President Everett's predecessor and President Russo of the Texas Territory. The treaty guaranteed no harm, but also stopped all financial support the US and Texas Territory had been giving the Colorado Territory. The treaty was crafted exactly as Case wanted. The Colorado Territory was free of all government, regulation, and laws. Case knew governance as the enemy of liberty.

Throughout history, the government only succeeded in growing strife for the very people it purported to protect. The two, government and liberty, could never live harmoniously.

"You know I can stop this attack that is coming diplomatically. I've done it before," Case said.

"We are beyond the point of diplomacy. The United States is in a deep depression, and President Everett has convinced its weary citizens that taking the Colorado Territory back will invigorate their stagnant economy," Reed said, placing his hand on his chin as if he was an economics teacher and Case was his student. "The movement is called *Rec-la-ma-tion*," he finished, iterating the word slowly.

Case pondered the word's frightening connotations—it meant taking his land back at any cost, including lives. "It doesn't have to be this way," he said. Case certainly wasn't going to let liberty end here, in an underground room within the very boundaries of Colorado. The only question now was how he was going to get out of this situation. "Just let me go so I can talk to—"

"You are less than nothing to Everett," Reed interrupted. "He sees us all as animals, nuisance animals for that matter, grazing off his land. He will neutralize and sterilize us. I'm afraid your attempts at talking will only make matters worse. It's why you are here now. I am stopping you from any discussions with the United States. You are putting more lives at risk."

"I just need to talk with them," Case said. "We've got to do something. If we do nothing, then we all die—and that includes you."

Reed put his palms flat on the folding table and leaned in, his head mere inches from Case's face. Reed's hot breath smelled like a musty old cabin. He displayed no nerves and clearly felt in control. "Oh, I don't intend to die, Mr. Tappan," Reed said. His tone was dark and sinister.

Case inhaled and tried to still his quivering hands. "Look at what you've accomplished," Case said. "Don't you think the ability to bring electricity to the Colorado Territory makes this place a target? What makes you so confident you aren't first on his list?"

"I have something to offer, don't you think?" Reed said, pulling away from Case. As Reed walked around Case, his shadow crept across the white table like a thundercloud.

Case fidgeted in his chair, sweat beading on his forehead and trickling down his temple. The light above him crackled with electricity and flickered briefly. "I don't know what you're talking about," Case said, but inside he knew if he were turned over to the United States as a prisoner, Reed would become the titular head of the Colorado Territory.

"Mr. Tappan," Reed said. "I can see the understanding in your eyes. You know exactly what I'm talking about. You're the prize and you know it. Everett would love to see you in prison."

"Don't," Case said. "I'm on your side."

"Maybe he'd torture you," Reed said, as an eerie grin stretched across his face. "Not just for the photo-op, but maybe for fun too."

Case looked at his hands, dry and chapped. He had spent four years proving to the world there was a different way. That civilization could be sustainable, peaceful, and prosperous without the need for money and profit. The Colorado Territory was a naturally-evolved system that efficiently delivered the essentials. The populace provided all that was ever needed and nothing that was unnecessarily wanted. Case never figured freedom would be anything less than a bonfire of inspiration. Now it was clear President Everett perceived the success of the Colorado Territory as a threat to what the United States had become—a dark society plagued by greed.

Case rose from his seat; his chair abruptly clanking to the floor. "You're making a mistake," he said. "If what you say is true, and we are nothing more than animals, why do you think he'd spare you?"

Reed stood in front of the exit. His stocky frame took up nearly the entire doorway. He wasn't going to budge. "I think he'd spare me," Reed said, "if I could deliver the very face of the movement he claims to have stolen his land, don't you think? Oh, your face would be on every newscast. The mere image of you in captivity would give Everett and the citizens of the United States much-needed assurance that they could return to greatness."

"That's not what will happen," Case retorted. "I have new ideas."

"Nobody needs your ideas anymore," Reed said, "I can deliver more than ideas. I can provide something tangible to the

Colorado Territory, like electricity. I will become the face that saved the lives of the Colorado Territory, not you." Reed inched away from the exit and stood close to Case. "But time is running short, Mr. Tappan. The Reclamation has already begun."

2

Callie Stanton opened her eyes and stretched her arms out to the early morning sun as its rays crept across the barren walls of her small house, which Callie called her living space. She rose and walked to the window. Sunrises in Eads, Colorado are stunning; the clouds and sun usually synchronized, creating a palatable pink hue, but today was different. Low-hanging clouds moved about the horizon, chased away by the sun's intense orange light. Instead of harmony, the sun challenged the clouds to a battle of perseverance, and the clouds looked more like they were on fire rather than cotton candy. Callie shielded her eyes and turned away from the window.

For the past four years, this self-sufficient community on the Eastern Plains was her home. She and her sister, Heather, came here in search of rectitude when the brutal and bloody battle between the United States and Texas raged in her hometown of Amarillo. Now, the United States and the Reclamation Movement had set their sights on Colorado. She was reassured by the fact that Case left town a day ago in an attempt to negotiate with President Everett. By now, he'd be close to the Kansas border. She knew they'd listen to him; they had before.

Callie left her space and moved casually to her barn where her horse, Abby, anxiously pawed the ground for food and attention. Abby was always a friend when Callie needed one. She took her out of the barn, found some hay, and gently hand-fed Abby a few bites before tossing the rest on the ground. As Abby ate, Callie gently opened the creaky door of the rickety tack room where she was met with the familiar, warm smell of aged barn wood. She rummaged through a chest that contained grooming items for Abby until she found a mane brush. She returned to Abby and brushed the wiry mane of her beloved horse. Abby loved the attention and nickered happily. Eads wasn't always an easy place to call home, but for Callie life within Eads was freeing and fulfilling. It was a life built around the core necessities of soul and family, versus that of extravagance.

In the distance, there was the sound of a loud retort, like a gunshot. Abby's ears perked up and she huffed heavy breaths through her nose. Callie hadn't heard a gunshot in years. No one she knew in Eads owned a weapon. "What was that?"

Callie looked toward the horizon and was met by the heavy rays of the scorching sun and what appeared to be a puff of smoke. Perhaps it was just another dust storm high on the rolling hills of the Eastern Plains. Dust storms kicked up on occasion, twirling about like miniature tornadoes. They had a distinctive brown hue, but this one was white and wispy. Smoke meant only one thing—fire. With heat like this, a fire was perfectly feasible, but there would be more lingering smoke, and perhaps even a subtle change to the way the air smelled.

Abby resumed eating but looked up with every bite. As the smoke dissipated into the hot air, Callie's skin prickled with chill and her gaze shifted about the land for more signs of danger. Familiar dirt roads etched the parched plains of Eads like outstretched fingers. Peaks of cottonwood trees poked their sizable heads from the depths of ravines like playful toddlers.

The occasional patch of purple alfalfa flowers provided a pop of color to the otherwise banal prairie grasses. The breathtaking panoramas and glass sky felt to Callie as if she were in a snow globe, and yet she had an eerie sensation it was about to be shaken.

She wasn't the only one. Her neighbors exited their living spaces, glancing east toward the blazing sun. Abby huffed and pawed at the ground. Callie placed Abby back in the barn, shut her in, and secured the door so the nervous horse would not be distracted by whatever was in the air this morning.

Callie walked down the dirt path where she found her sister. Heather's gaze darted back and forth. Her face was pale, and she looked as if she hadn't slept at all.

"Everything okay?" Callie asked.

"Something's up, Cal," Heather said. "Henry and Buck went out a while ago to get eggs for breakfast."

At seven years old Heather's son, Henry, loved two things— collecting eggs in the morning and Buck, his German Shepherd. It was the life a seven-year-old should have. His was a life that was pure, simple and connected with other living entities. Connection with nature was why Heather decided to take Henry to Colorado. The alternative would have meant Henry faced growing up surrounded by the brutality of civil war.

"Probably just Buck chasing a jackrabbit," Callie said. "Sometimes he gets too far away."

"I don't know," Heather replied. "I heard Buck barking kind of aggressively. Now, he's stopped. Will you come with me, just over the hill?"

"Of course," Callie responded. Her sister was there for her. Coming to Colorado with her was not an easy decision but their older brother Aaron insisted they leave Texas in order to protect them. The People's War, as Aaron referred to it, started when the United States took up arms against the people of Amarillo. It was the battle that ultimately led to the Second Civil War.

Aaron was obsessed with the war. He served Texas admirably,

leading the People's Army to such a commanding victory that when a new government was formed in Texas, President Russo named him the defense secretary. As Aaron grew closer to the central power of a large government, he grew further apart from his sisters. When the opportunity to return to Texas came, Callie and Heather chose to stay in Colorado.

Callie and Heather started toward the eastern hills. The hotness of the morning was so strong that the sun may well have been able to ignite the dry grassland. The aromatic scent of sage tickled Callie's nose, and her shoulders slumped in the heat as she and Heather pressed on.

"Buck," Heather shouted. "Can you hear me, boy?"

"Henry," Callie called out. Their voices seemed echoless and died in the blistering air.

Ahead, Callie noticed an object sprawled awkwardly on the ground. "What's that?" she asked.

Heather looked and shook her head. "I don't know," she said and squinted her eyes. "I think it's an animal of some kind."

"It's the size of a dog," Callie said and ran to the object.

"Buck!" Heather screamed as they approached the dog.

He was breathing heavy shallow breaths; his pink tongue almost touched the ground as it hung from his mouth. Buck's fur was wet, and when Callie touched him her hand was coated in blood from a significant hole near his chest.

"Jesus," Callie muttered.

"What happened?" Heather asked in a high-pitched voice. "Buck," she shouted again.

"I don't understand," Callie said. "This hole looks like a gunshot."

"Who would do that?" Heather asked. "We can save him."

There was too much blood. "Heather," Callie said. "He's dead."

Heather kneeled by her friend and sobbed. She clutched her fists and didn't move. "We have to find Henry."

"I know," Callie said. She reached out and hugged her

sister tightly. "He's okay. Henry's just frightened and hiding somewhere. We'll find him."

Callie and Heather moved quickly, looking behind every tree and rock they could find. Callie spotted a person atop a hill. "Over there," Callie pointed.

"Henry," Callie called out and waved her arms. Alas, it was not Henry. It was Elizabeth, their neighbor. Her face was pale, and she staggered as she walked toward them as if inebriated.

"Elizabeth," Callie said as she took her into her arms. "What's happened?"

"Callie," Elizabeth said. "It's the Reclamation. They've got a bunch of us who were out this morning. Just over the hill."

"Is Henry there?" Heather asked.

"I don't know," Elizabeth said.

"I'm going," Heather said. "You stay with Elizabeth."

"Don't," Elizabeth said. "You'll be trapped. We have to warn the others."

"He's my son," Heather said. "I'm not going to leave him." She ran toward the hill.

"They've rounded them all up, Callie," Elizabeth cried. "They aren't here to negotiate. We have to warn everyone. We have to get out."

Callie watched as Heather raced toward the hill. She couldn't let her sister face this alone. "Go warn as many people as you can, Elizabeth," Callie said. "I have to go."

"Don't," Elizabeth said.

"I have no choice," Callie said. Elizabeth nodded and ran toward Eads.

As Callie watched Elizabeth run, the distinct din of a diesel vehicle grabbed her attention. It sounded like the distant grumble of a hungry monster. Along the northeast horizon, the dark shadow of a truck crept closer toward Callie's beloved home. Two more vehicles crested the red horizon, taking on the appearance of the ghoulish head of Hydra. Behind her, more vehicles approached from the south. She was surrounded; her idyllic view of her land collapsing fast.

At that moment, Callie heard Heather's scream. Callie raced toward her sister's distressed call. She crested the hill and stopped. American soldiers had lined people up and forced them to their knees. One was Henry, and another was Heather. A soldier spotted Callie and pointed his weapon at her. She came toward them and kneeled next to her sister.

Within moments, six heavy-duty white trucks marked with the flag of the United States crawled over the hill and stopped. The formerly proud flag once stood as a beacon of liberty and expression of free will. An icon of a great nation that Callie once believed could free the globe from the ailments of corruption, greed, and the malfeasance of financial misappropriation draped over the weakened backs of the poor.

Instead, the rule of law succumbed to the power of persuasion. America's government feasted on the fleshy meat of freedom, taking it from citizens in exchange for rations of food and money. The rise of such inhumanity masqueraded as a generous heap of liberty, yet served only to enslave individuality, prosperity, and faith behind the dark iron cages of a lost ideology.

Case recognized any society built of money would eventually suffer the same consequences. The Colorado Territory was conceived as cashless commerce. Those who created objects or works of art did so for pure gratification and nothing else in return. Much to the vexation of a president beholden to the selfish and unenlightened, this concept of freedom was working. America had finally collapsed under the weight of its own greed. As a result, the government forced its citizens into despair and hunger by taking every earned dollar. Now the United States sought to fill its empty stomach with the lives of those within the Colorado Territory; innocent lives who aspired to cast an antiquated vision of society into its final resting spot of history once and for all.

From the cold, steel beds of those American trucks emerged

soldiers of the army, dressed in familiar green camouflage. They methodically lined up facing the kneeling innocents of Eads. There was an eerie silence as if the soldiers' larynges had been ripped out of their gullets in an attempt to quell the voices of dissent.

These were the empty faces of soldiers with the blank stares and darkened souls of a humanity aborted, sent to perform the bidding of their leader. President Everett viewed the inhabitants of the Colorado Territory as heathens upending the ironic tranquility of dictatorship.

One soldier bore the task of standing with an automatic rifle by his side while holding the United States flag in his burly hands. Now Callie viewed the red within the flag as a reflection of bloodletting and revenge.

The day of revenge appeared to be upon them now, as the general of the troop spoke. "Well," he said, with a deep voice of disdain. "What have we here?"

"Leave us alone," Callie said, stoically. She spoke because she believed in this community, and she loved Case.

The general smiled. His mouth was filled with yellow teeth. Remnants of chaw were visibly trapped within their crooked spaces. His skin was wrinkled at the eyes and his leathery appearance showed no affection or mercy.

"I recognize you," The general said. "I believe you are Ms. Callie Stanton."

Callie's stomach twisted and the world seemed to spin. She didn't respond but stared straight into his eyes.

"It's okay," The general said. "I know who you are. I should tell you that we've located your boyfriend, Case, near the border. It appears he was trying to bring electricity to you. We can't allow that, now can we?" The general stared at Callie. "I can see you're frightened. Not to worry, dear. It won't be long before all of this is over."

Callie looked to her left where she was met by the eyes of her friends. Henry shivered in his mother's arms. Heather blinked at Callie, silently begging for help. Callie had to act. "We are nothing but peaceful and we do no harm," she said.

"No harm? Is this so? Well, President Everett and I couldn't disagree more. You have stolen from us."

"Stolen what?" Callie asked.

"As if you don't know," The general replied. The metal adornments on his uniform clanked as his shoulders pitched with his laughter. "You stole our resources. This very land is our access to plenty. The ground you stand on has everything we need to remake our society. You stole our farmlands. You stole our mountains. You stole our access to oil and the roads across the plains. And we are here to reclaim them so the people of the United States can once again prosper."

"Our land is not yours to reclaim," Callie said. "The United States signed a treaty with the Colorado Territory. "Violation will cost you."

"Cost us what, Ms. Stanton? Hmm? We've nothing left," The general said.

"If it's land you want, let these believers go," Callie said.

The general smiled and looked at the lineup. In total there were three dozen people. "Very well," he said. "Stand up," he ordered the citizens.

They obliged. Heather reached out and held her shaking son's hand. She tried to appear calm, but her gaze darted about and she stumbled when she stood up.

"Let them walk away," Callie said.

"This should be more fun anyhow," he said. "Did I forget to mention we've got Eads surrounded?"

With that, he raised his right arm. When he did, the soldiers raised their weapons, their bores as cold as the eyes of the soldiers holding them.

Callie knew when his arm came down the bullets would follow. "Run!" was all she could manage to yell as she turned and bolted.

The gunfire was deafening. Her friends were easy targets in

the open field. Callie felt bullets whiz by her body and waited for the searing pain of a direct hit, but it didn't come. The deep howls of men and the unruly high-pitched wails of women filled the air. These were the sounds of horror and painful death. Automatic rifles fired rapidly.

Callie ran. Her legs raced harder, but her lungs heaved so fast they burned. She needed a moment, a second to catch her breath and gain her bearings. Up ahead was an empty shell of an abandoned Jeep and she ducked behind it.

Callie peered around the Jeep and directly into the faces of her enemy. She witnessed ugliness unleashed. The rules of engagement may well have been written on flash paper. Animal soldiers lunged at innocent people with territorial aggression and plunged a hail of bullets into the backs of fleeing bodies. She watched as a person hit the ground face first. His body bounced once and then lay still.

As bodies fell to the ground like windblown autumn leaves, Heather called out to Callie. The bloody tracks of bullets tore open a gaping wound along her scalp. A mere inch down and the bullet would have extracted her brain with an explosive exit. A raw, red-tinged bone jutted awkwardly from her right leg.

"Callie," Heather said. The beleaguered breath of death was evident.

"Heather," Callie whispered because fear took her voice away. "No."

Callie ran to her sister and kneeled by her body.

"Go to the bunker," Heather said. "We need you to survive."

The bunker was built to protect a connection to the outside world in the event of an emergency, and this certainly qualified. That connection was a computer linked to a random satellite. Callie's body jerked with heavy tearful sobs. She tried to compose herself but couldn't. "This is my fault," Callie said. "I want to die with you."

"No Callie," Heather pleaded. "Don't give up. I saw Henry run away. He could be alive. I need you now. Please. This movement became my heart and soul. I'm a believer and I'll die for this cause. Don't you let it be in vain." Heather's body slumped, as the vibrancy within her eyes disappeared. Blood encircled her eyelids and streaked down her face like a final epitaph of red symbols. The stories of freedom were once again quelled with bullets. Callie watched her only sister die. It had been a while since Callie had talked to God and perhaps it was too late now, but she lowered her head and prayed. Faith in God's way was the only hand she could hold now, but there was a wave of silent anger that swelled in her stomach. She clenched her fist in a tight ball, wiped tears from her face, and withheld her screams so she would not be heard. It was time to move on.

The bunker was ten feet behind her, but bullets swept through the air and the thick stench of smoke from nearby fires obscured the skies. Even if she got there alive, she'd have to somehow pry open the heavy, steel bunker door. She never imagined she'd have to do it alone.

She inhaled deeply. The smoke made her dizzy and her mind rejected what her eyes just witnessed. Callie was in shock as her mind searched for a way to make sense of the violence and gore that surrounded her. She had to get to the bunker.

Callie rose and ran to the underground bunker. Through heavy layers of smoke, members of the US Army took on the appearance of combatants. They were no longer concerned about the reclamation of land, but the need to kill as many people as possible. As if taking land wasn't enough, these soldiers emphasized their actions by placing bullets into the very soul of liberty's believers. She heard gunfire and saw a bullet explode the head of a resident in a splattering of blood and gray matter. Forever silenced.

She was five feet away from safety, the cement door to the bunker within reach. "Over here," a voice shouted.

Heavy footsteps ran toward her. She dropped to the ground, stopped moving and lay in the grass. Pretending to be dead wasn't a stretch; it already felt as if she were. Everything she stood for was destroyed by the need to advance a government-sponsored utopia.

"They're on the run," a soldier said.

"We got most of those fucks," a second soldier replied. There was a lull in the action as the two men stood near Callie's motionless body. If she showed any signs of life she'd surely be shot in the back. She pictured herself standing and screaming at them. She wanted to defend her land so badly. The humiliation of lying prone, face in the dirt, was unbearable and her body shook, not with fear, but with rage. Unimaginable thoughts sparked within her. If she had a weapon, she'd use it. There was no longer a doubt in her mind. She saw herself rising from the grass and deploying bullets into the hearts of these demented soldiers. Just getting two of them would give her great pleasure. She knew at that moment what needed to happen. She wasn't going to allow her land to be reclaimed. She was going to stop them before they could strike again. Stop them on their own land. She was going to fight.

After what seemed like an eternity, the soldiers moved away and Callie took her chance. She slithered slowly to the bunker door and tried to pry it open with her hands while on the ground. The door was too heavy and wouldn't budge. She needed to stand for leverage. She noticed a uniformed soldier about two hundred yards to her west. His back faced her.

She glanced at the sky. The sun had barely moved from the time Callie noticed the first diesel truck. It struck her how fast everything changed. Four years of diplomacy ended by ten minutes of violence.

Callie rose to her feet and wrapped both hands around the iron handle of the sunbaked bunker door. She needed to pull and slide the door in one fluid motion. She inhaled and twisted the door ajar with a loud sound. The nearby soldier turned and looked at Callie. He raised his rifle. Callie slipped into the bunker as shots fired. She hoped like hell the guard thought he struck her. She reached up, slid the door shut, and locked it into place.

There was just enough light leaking through the hatch to see. She was eight short steps down the ladder and a few feet from the emergency computer. There was only one person Callie could think of to contact—her brother, Aaron. Callie took a moment to catch her breath as she came to terms with what seemed like her inevitable death.

Callie stumbled her way in the dark to the laptop and lifted the screen. The soft light lit up the small space, and with the light came hope. As the computer booted, she noted the satellite connection was there, but the battery life was only ten percent. The computer was solar-powered, and she could not risk leaving the bunker to recharge it.

With no time to waste, she established a direct video communication link to Aaron's phone, which Callie knew he manned religiously. There was a crackle and a hiss, but there was no video.

"Aaron," Callie said. "Can you hear me? We are under attack by the United States and I am in danger. I need your help. Aaron? Can you hear me?"

The computer teased her with hints of connectivity and thinly veiled noises that occasionally sounded like a human being. Suddenly, Aaron's hazy face appeared on the scrambled screen.

"Aaron, did you hear me?" Callie yelled into the computer.

"Cal— are— hurt?" Her brother's voice crackled in and out of range and echoed against the concrete walls.

"No. I just made it," she said. "But Heather is dead, and I don't know if Henry survived. Aaron. I'm scared. We need you." She thought of Heather's dying words—*Don't let me die in vain.*

"I need Texas to help to stop this," she pleaded. She had to plead. This wasn't an easy request to ask of her brother. He was technically an adversary of the United States and helping the Colorado Territory would be akin to waging war against the United States. Another full-fledged civil war could easily break out.

The video link made a noise that reminded Callie of a trapped cat. The battery life ticked down like seconds, five percent left now.

"Aaron, help me," Callie said again. Suddenly the connection improved, and so too did the battery consumption—three percent. Aaron's face flickered into focus. The years following the civil war had taken its toll on him. Deep wrinkles etched his forehead with linear design, and his eyes no longer seemed sharp and vivid. She recalled the face of her teenaged younger brother. It seemed impossible this weathered looking person on the screen was the same person.

"Jesus," was all that Aaron managed to say as he lowered his head.

"Can you get me?" Callie asked.

"It's too risky to get you in Eads right now," Aaron said. "Do you think you can get to the Texas border?"

"That's too far, Aaron," Callie said. "I don't have a car,"

"Crossing the border is an act of war. I know you need help, but discretion is my first order of business."

Callie was surprised at Aaron's ability to sack his emotions and stay focused.

"Christ Callie, I could be removed from office for this, you know. It's a breach of the treaty. Treason comes with penalties."

The battery was at one percent.

"Be here in two days," Aaron continued. "I'll have a car ready and waiting on the corner of Canterberry and Daliah Street by Daisy's Market. Please be safe. I'll pray for you," Aaron added at the end. He sounded sincere.

"But that's not possible on foot. I need twice that. Please." Callie started. The computer blinked and shut off. Infinite darkness filled the bunker.

3

"Callie?" Aaron said into his phone. "Callie, are you still there?" He had heard most of what Callie had said but desperately wanted to know more.

The call ended and he noticed his reflection in the screen of his computer. His eyebrows were high on his forehead and his mouth was agape. He may well have been looking at the face of a stranger he didn't want to know. He placed the phone screen side down onto his mahogany office desk and rubbed his forehead with the palms of his hands.

A black, leather-bound Bible lay innocently at the corner of his desk. He reached over, slid the sacred book close and tapped on the front cover. When he was thirteen years old, Heather and Callie gave him this Bible for confirmation. He slowly opened the front cover and read the inscription inside.

Aaron, we are so proud of you. May God bless you always. Love, Heather, and Callie.

He recognized the playful way Heather crossed the T in her name. The T curled upward and reminded him of a wave about to break. He riffled the thin pages of the Bible with his thumb, knowing there would be some text to help him cope with his grief. He flipped to Psalms, but the words didn't help much. The time for reflection would have to be later. He closed his Bible and returned it to its position on his desk.

He thumbed a tear away from the corner of his eye and fought the urge to produce more. "Damn it," he mumbled aloud, pounding his fist on his desk.

The loud thump echoed off the walls of his office within the confines of the Territory Capitol Building. His office was that of the secretary of defense for the Texas Territory, which included the former states of Texas, South Carolina, Georgia, Alabama, Kentucky, Tennessee, Arkansas, Mississippi, and Louisiana.

He clenched his fists and closed his eyes as he recalled the moment everything changed four years ago. He had been eating breakfast, scrolling through news feeds, when he saw two headlines that tore apart the pillars that stabilized his life. US Congress had passed both an ordinance labeling the Catholic Church a hate group, and a federal law labeling gun owners as criminals unless they turned their weapons over to federal agents.

Aaron knew it was time to exercise his civic duty. He joined a group of protesters who had formed outside the Capitol Building in Amarillo. When the first bullets flew into the crowd, he thought they were fireworks, until the screaming began. As the crowd dispersed, he scrambled for cover too. He had not carried his weapon and being unable to defend himself was terrifying; a feeling reserved for the dark recesses of his mind. He vowed that would never happen again, and soon he became the face of the Second Civil War and the People's Army.

Aaron opened his eyes. The mere memory of that day caused his body to tremble. He rose and paced his office. On his wall hung the original *Washington Post* article with pictures of his role in the Battle of Amarillo. The headline read "Texas's Last Stand" and included an action photograph of the People's Army aiming rifles at the very Capitol Building he now occupied. The United States Congress condemned the event as an act of war, and the country chose sides. Aaron knew where his loyalties lay, but Callie and Heather were still undecided. Aaron didn't want to see them hurt. He sent them to Colorado for safety, but when the war ended, neither wanted to return home to Texas. He pursed his lips and looked away from the article.

On the far wall was a picture of him and President Russo of Texas during the secession ceremony which officially separated the southern states from the control of the US government. The act freed Texas to form its own government. Former Texas Governor Duane Russo was elected president of the Texas Territory, and he appointed Aaron the secretary of defense.

Aaron took the picture from the wall and held it tightly to him. He sighed, recalling that he had invited Callie and Heather to the ceremony, but neither came. They were both involved with creating a new land of their own in Colorado.

Aaron placed the picture back on the wall above one of himself on an oil rig anchored in the depths of the Gulf shores. In the four years since secession had passed, the oil-rich economy of the Texas Territory thrived while the economy of the United States suffered. Last year the angry citizens of the US went to the polls and elected pro-Reclamation candidate Ray Everett by a large margin.

Aaron took the picture of the oil rig from the wall and cringed at the memory it evoked. Ray Everett had been a good friend and former member of the Texas legislative body. In the months before the start of the Second Civil War, they met once in a musty meeting room. Having served as a general in the US Army, Everett arrived for the meeting in full uniform. He spoke in condescending tones and demanded that the People's Army disband. When Aaron refused, Everett told him, "I will make you regret this decision." Everett subsequently quit his post at the legislature and started campaigning for president in the US.

Aaron opened his desk drawer and slid the picture face

down into the rear of the drawer. The darkness behind Everett's words echoed in his mind. Was he coming for Aaron's family as a form of revenge? Was the Reclamation personal? Was it only a coincidence that the movement began in Eads, where Aaron's sisters lived? His stomach soured with a sensation of rotten remorse. He felt responsible for Heather's death.

He walked to the window and stared at the grounds of the Capitol. The grounds were beautifully manicured and serene, but it didn't take his mind away from his thoughts. He pushed the drapes partially shut and walked to his bookshelf where he kept the Medal of Courage awarded to him for his role in the civil war. He picked up the twenty-four-karat gold medal. He caressed the satisfyingly hefty weight of the medal in his palm. He earned this gold. He had led several successful brigades to victory over the United States. He had lost men, but he'd never lost a battle.

Still holding the medal, Aaron found his phone on his desk and scrolled through the contact list. His thumb stopped on the name "Russo." Paralyzing nerves in his fingers tried to prevent him from making the call, but he needed to brief the president. Aaron called the line and placed his phone on speaker.

"Duane Russo," the president said, his deep voice piercing the relative silence of Aaron's office.

Aaron opened his mouth, but nothing came out.

"Mr. Stanton?" Russo said.

"Sir," Aaron managed. "I need to make you aware of a situation."

"A situation?"

"Yes. The United States launched an attack within the Colorado Territory."

"Okay," Russo replied. The banal tone to his voice suggested a lack of interest.

Aaron's gaze shifted around the room. He was expecting more of a response. "The attack occurred at Eads."

"Has there been a threat to Texas?" Russo asked.

"Not directly," Aaron said.

"Thank you for letting me know," Russo said. "Monitor the situation and keep me appraised if the status changes. Are people dead?" He asked as if an afterthought.

Aaron closed his eyes. "Yes," he responded softly. "Many have been killed, including my sister, Heather, and probably her only son."

Aaron heard the change in Russo's breathing, but the man didn't respond immediately.

"I am very sorry for your loss," Duane said. He was about as empathetic as Aaron had ever heard him. "Please let me know if there is anything you need in terms of accommodations."

"Actually," Aaron responded, "there is something I need."

"Go on," Duane said. "Anything."

"My other sister Callie survived the attack. I believe she is being targeted by Everett as a form of revenge. She has asked to come to Texas and stay with me."

"I see," Duane said, hesitation evident in his voice. "Is her stay permanent?"

"I see no reason for her to go back," Aaron said. "Is there a problem?"

"I know that she is your family. But does she support the ideals of Texas?" Russo asked.

"She—" Aaron stopped. Callie never came home when the war ended, and what bothered Aaron most is she never explained as to why. If he was to help her, she at least owed him one now. "She needs help. I don't think she would have called if she wasn't willing to integrate. I can work with her."

"Mr. Stanton, with all due respect, I am aware of her abandonment of Texas. She is involved with Case Tappan and the formation of the Colorado Territory. You yourself felt she abandoned both faith and country," Russo said. "We both know where her loyalties lie. She yields a certain amount of influence, and I do not want that influence to permeate Texas."

Aaron's hand gripped the phone so hard it hurt. "What

choice does she have? It's that or die."

"Should she not stay and fight for what she believes in, Aaron? You didn't flee when the sovereignty of Texas was at stake. If she is not willing to die for Colorado, would she live for Texas?"

Aaron's leg shook and he scratched his brow. He wished like hell that he never mentioned Callie at all. As much as he wanted to tell Russo she would live for Texas, he doubted she would.

"I don't know," Aaron said. "But she is my sister, and somewhere in there is the sister who once lived for Texas. I just need to find her again."

After a pause, Russo asked, "Is it just her?"

"Yes," Aaron replied.

"I tell you what. I will allow temporary asylum for your sister under this set of extraordinary circumstances," Russo said. "But I cannot allow everyone fleeing the Colorado Territory into Texas. The people there are— How do I say this politely? Different. We can't have Texas become Colorado. If she is to stay permanently, you must get a commitment from her that she is willing to salute and promote our great flag."

Aaron clenched his jaw. He walked to the window, peeled back the drapes, and observed the flag of Texas high up a pole in the center of the Capitol gardens. He was proud of the flag. He had lost men for that emblem, and it was the most important symbol of his life. He abided by its standards. "I understand. I can make that happen. Sir, I have one more question."

"Go ahead," Russo said.

"Is there reason for concern?"

"Concern for what?" Russo asked.

"Increased aggression from the United States?" Aaron responded.

"Mr. Stanton, you are my advisor and I place a great deal of trust into your ability to analyze situations. I expect you to tell me if there is reason for concern. So, allow me to ask the question. Should we be worried?"

Aaron looked far into the clear blue horizon of the afternoon, half expecting to see United States Air Force jets emerging from the distance targeting the Capitol. The People's Army managed to stand firm against the significantly stronger army of the United States, but that was in large part due to a lack of willingness of the United States to obliterate Texas.

Things were different now. The US economy was in disrepair, and Ray Everett fueled anger by suggesting the people within the Colorado Territory were the reason there was no food on the tables of American citizens. He stoked fear by suggesting they were the reason there was no gas for American's cars. He built support by suggesting the only reasonable solution was to retrieve the land from the savages who stole it.

"Mr. Stanton," Russo prodded. "I am waiting for an answer."

"Any direct threats against Texas will be met with a resilience and bravery like you've never seen, sir. Should the need occur, our men will rise to the challenge. I don't think that time is now. I will let you know should the situation escalate." Aaron answered.

"Very well. I've put my faith in you, Aaron." It always made Aaron feel better when Russo used his first name. "You've never let the good people of Texas down. May God continue to bless our land and our great flag."

"Thank you," Aaron answered and ended the call.

Russo had a soft spot, and Aaron knew it. But one misstep could set Russo off, and whoever offended him saw the end of their political career. Aaron worked hard in his role and he wasn't going to let his career slip away, even for his sister.

Aaron scrolled through the contacts on his phone and called his security detail, Lindsey Nichols. "My sister, Callie Stanton fled Colorado and has been granted asylum by Russo. Can you prepare a car and retrieve her in Stratford?"

"Shouldn't we retrieve her in Colorado?" Nichols asked.

"I wish we could, but it is too risky to extricate her. The United States occupied the territory and the situation is volatile.

I do not wish to entice retaliation. I feel horrible, but she will have to make the journey on foot. Be prepared to pick her up and make her comfortable," Aaron said.

"Okay," Nichols responded. "We'll be there. How long should we wait if she's not there?"

Aaron shuddered at the notion she may not make it at all. "She'll get there when she gets there," he said and ended the call.

He walked to the window and drew the drapes closed. He returned to his desk and lowered his head into his hands. He took a moment to cry for Heather. He failed her and her son and he would break completely if Callie didn't arrive safely.

He folded his hands together, closed his eyes tight, and prayed to God for guidance.

4

Case inched closer to the door as Reed slowly walked the perimeter of the white holding cell. Maybe if the door were open, he could just run.

"There's nowhere to go. I've sealed all the exits," Reed said, apparently reading Case's body language. "You're in a fortified underground village. This is where the brains of Project Grid are safe."

Case moved away from the door. How he got here had been a blur. Only a few hours ago, he was on his way to the US border in Kansas when he was intercepted, taken into this building, and led down a set of stairs.

"I was told that President Everett would like to thank me personally for delivering you," Reed said. "He offered me a reward, of course. Well, it's more of an investment in Project Grid. This will change everything. I will bring the Colorado Territory back into the twenty-first century."

"You won't be allowed to use your energy," Case said. "Everett only wants to shut you up. Are you willing to trade your freedom to the United States?"

Reed smiled. "I see," he said. "You seem to think your little experiment with freedom is working, don't you?"

"My 'little experiment'?" Case said. "I can assure you liberty is not an experiment, it's a right."

"Without governance, liberty only serves as a pathway to poverty," Reed replied.

"Poverty is unique to all forms of economic systems, and I believe it is by design of the government."

"So, you think cashless commerce is the solution?" Reed asked.

"I'm proposing the use of something far more valuable than cash," Case said. "I believe everything has a value, but it does not need to be quantified with money. Think of it as the evolution of capitalism. Ask yourself—If money didn't exist for whatever reason—be it disease, nuclear war, an ice age, what would happen to us? Would we erupt in a frenzy of rage and turn into angry hoarders? I say we wouldn't. I say we would continue to meet the demands of modern society regardless of money,"

"Life is not sustainable unless there is money."

Case glanced at Reed's stone-cold eyes. "Why are you even here then? You didn't have to choose Colorado."

"To make a better world," Reed said. "But there's no incentive to make advancements. I've found myself doing vast amounts of labor for no reward. And we're being left behind by the rest of the world."

"Left behind from what?"

"Advancement in technology has surpassed every expectation, yet here we are in Colorado seeking simple electricity."

"I understand," Case said. "But tell me how are we advancing as a society? Why do you assume if there was no money that we'd return to the dark ages? Would all of our accumulated knowledge suddenly disappear? Would we instantly abandon our pursuits of technological advancements and make fire with two sticks? I say we wouldn't. In fact, we may even pursue them more aggressively in order to maintain the life we've grown accustomed to. But they would be only the things that matter, as there would be no time for the frivolous excess that has consumed our minds. The reduction in wasteful ventures would streamline our thoughts and resources into efficiently producing that which is necessary. Don't you see that?"

"But money gives inventors freedom to think of more inventions," Reed argued.

"So, if it weren't for the promise of money, you would not want to bring electricity to Colorado?" Case asked.

"What would be the point?" Reed replied. "There would be no logical reason to do so."

"Then you are not advancing anything," Case shot back. "For the most part, we as a society are only chasing the dollar. This once-proud system only serves two things: money-hungry, power-driven politicians, and advancing the demise of human intelligence by flooding the market with that which is unnecessary. Chasing profits fuels false advertising, class warfare, and racism. When corporations lie in bed with politicians, it suppresses the fundamental right of freedom. Tell me—If you could cure diseases, but were promised no money, would you continue your research?"

"My time and effort ought to be rewarded," Reed said.

"So, for you, there is no value in saving lives?" Case asked as he sat down.

Reed put his hands on the table and leaned in. "This condescending belief that you've got it all figured out is exactly why President Everett thinks the believers in Colorado are backward."

Case shook his head. "Don't be so naive. If the money is gone then so is Everett's power. When the power is gone, so is the control. You are jealous of him. You are the one going backward. I can tell you with certainty that Everett is not interested in sharing any of his power with you. Once he gets what he wants, you'll be sent curbside."

"You have no idea," Reed said, his fists clenched tight. "I hope I get to watch him torture you." Reed's face turned red, revealing his true hateful nature.

At that moment Case realized intolerance is no more than ideological ignorance. Liberty is fundamentally tolerant. If, however, one does not believe in liberty, then intolerance becomes the default position. Intolerance is a tool used by politicians to place people into groups in order to convince the masses that these groups hold the same ideology based on their characteristics. Once hatred of groups embeds itself, control, imprisonment, and death of the offenders are justifiable.

Suddenly, an explosion rocked the cell. The floor shook violently. Case closed his eyes and steadied himself. His body quivered so relentlessly his bones clacked against each other.

Reed's face flushed and he glanced around the room. He tried to open the door, but it refused to budge. "What the hell is going on?"

The room rumbled again and the lights flicked out, casting them into utter darkness. Another explosion ripped through the room, piercing Case's eardrums and rattling his brain. He crumbled to the floor in search of mercy. He shielded his eyes and braced himself for impact. The steel exit door blew off its hinges, filling the room with a blinding light.

Reed let loose a howl as his body hurtled backward across the holding cell. He hit the back wall with a sickening thud, like the sound of a heavy tree branch hitting the ground. The raw intensity of the explosion burned Case's exposed skin. A glow of hot orange fire coming through the doorway lit the room. Reed's contorted body lay on the floor; his neck twisted in such an impossible way that it could not be restrained any longer by muscles and vertebrae. Case searched Reed's face for any sign of life but found only gaping eye sockets filled with the red-and-white goop of melted eyeballs.

Case rose. The fortified cell walls remained intact and he

was still alive. He looked through the doorway. To his right were intense flames, and to his left, a great empty hall. The flames offered just enough light to see. The hallway retained heat like an oven and sweat poured from his brow. As he started up the hall, he searched the walls for an exit sign but saw none. He hurried, passing closed doors along the way.

As he maneuvered across a maze of rubble, his foot hit something hard and pain shot up his leg. He limped along as he tried to distance himself from the fire approaching behind him. With each painful step, he wondered if Eads suffered the same fate as this place.

He pictured Callie as he moved, and it encouraged him. He thought of how the appearance of her dark brown eyes offered stern fortitude with a touch of forgiveness when coupled with her smile. He thought of how she kept her ample figure hidden under jeans and frumpy shirts like a concealed weapon.

All his life he longed to be with someone just like her, and yet he resisted. He knew if he acted on these feelings, even for one sweaty night of animal fulfillment, those urges would cost them everything. Their work required focus and he could not afford to have his energy diverted by the spoils of adult yearnings. Giving in would make him weak, he would become one who could submit to idle temptations for the sake of convenience. If he had touched her even once, the foundation of their world would lie on a weak moment of impurity and hot desire. Theirs would be no different from the societies of generations past beholden to the intangible gods of immorality and corruption. Together they discussed how the Colorado Territory was a personhood of unique individuality; one of symbiosis without written doctrine, political or religious.

Oh, but if he could see her again. If he could see her one more time, he would let their conversation end with extended eye contact and that familiar smile. He'd reach out and tenderly hold her hand. She'd laugh and playfully toss her silky black hair away from her smooth forehead. They'd kiss in an open, sun-lit field as their bodies became one like their minds already were.

As smoke filled the air, Case focused on getting out. He reached the end of the hall, finding nothing but crumbled cement. In the eerie silence and dim light, his hollow breath echoed in the chamber that could become his tomb.

Case felt along the ragged, broken edges of the walls when a faint ray of light found its way through the rubble and darkness. The light danced in the dark like a happy child and captured the thickness of the smoke in its baroque beam. He slowly traced the beam with his finger, as if it contained magical powers. He traced the light to its origin—a crack in the cement. He picked up a chunk of rubble, pulled it over his head with both hands, and stood back. He closed his eyes and threw the heavy chunk at the embryonic ray. The rubble shattered, and when the dust settled, more light materialized through a crack now big enough to fit the tip of his fingers through. He pulled hard at the cement and a small bit fell to the floor.

As Case cast aside portion after portion, the heat became intolerable. He moved with the intensity of a locomotive. The sustained action tore the skin on his fingers and palms to shreds. Desperate for clean air, an agonizing cough followed each inhaled breath.

Case hauled cement aside until the hole was big enough for fresh air to pour in. He stuck his mouth to the hole and took in oxygen like a drug. He continued to push aside larger masses. His hands looked like red rags. Blood flowed and skin peeled away from his fortune lines.

Smoke found the gap and replaced the fresh air with a vile bouquet of ash. Case gagged, and his entire body ached. He had to sit down for a moment. He rested his head in his bloody palms. Soot and blood caressed his lips and it tasted like defeat.

In his mind, he sailed along a stream of fresh air. Pure bliss lifted the stress from his shoulders. There was an overwhelming sense of peaceful release as he accepted the inevitable death to come. He was ready to explore the ultimate freedom. He closed his eyes and prepared himself for his final breaths.

Instead, another explosion shook the hall. He was still alive. Maybe it was a second chance. Despite the pain, his brain convinced his body to move more cement. Finally, the hole became big enough to crawl through and he wasted no time basking in his impossible feat. He squeezed his body into the hole. His broad shoulders became stuck and he shrugged them as close to his neck as possible. As he pulled forward, toothed rock tore through his skin, leaving behind traces of skin and blood. His shoulders broke free and Case wailed as a stone dug jagged claws into his arms.

The remainder of his body passed with relative ease and Case found himself in a staircase. Blood stained his torn shirt and pants. An exit sign pointed up the stairs. Despite the pain, he managed a laugh, "There's the fucking sign." He limped up the stairs, came to a door hanging by one hinge, and burst out into fresh air.

Outside, windmills rose from the ground like towering, slender giants. Their size projected powerful, long shadows against a morning sun. Blades twirled majestically in an arbitrary wind and cut the air with the methodical cadence of a heartbeat. Project Grid was indeed no joke. Reed was truly ready to bring much-needed energy to the Colorado Territory. Now the windmills swung their useless arms in circles, producing nothing over and over again. Some windmills fell and others leaned precariously, their sturdy bases were torn agape.

Between a circle of turbines, the flag of the Colorado Territory flew. Its symbol was a merger of anarchy and peace sewn into the silky black fabric. Three slender, intersecting lines emerged from a circle and spread their roots. It signified enlightenment, not a national identity. Freedom is universal, and individuals left to their own devices, devoid of the burdens of institutional instruction, naturally strive toward a perfect society. The flag didn't need to be representative of any particular destination. The Colorado Territory was only where the flag flew, not what it represented.

Among a cemetery of fallen windmills, Case noticed a smoldering, gaping hole that penetrated deep into the ground. The windmills lay like dead soldiers in an army of steel. It became apparent to Case that he had survived a bombing. There was a loud rumble and another deafening boom.

Case held his ears as three jets rushed overhead. They were flying east and low enough to take out the tops of the windmills. In a flash, the jets of modern manifest destiny vanished beyond the smoky horizon. The Reclamation was upon him, but for the moment, the earth was silent. The only sound Case picked up was that of his dying flag flapping in a westerly prairie breeze.

5

The darkness of Callie's bunker caused her to break out in a cold sweat. Her skin felt as if bugs crept across her and parasites crawled through the folds of her brain, as she waited for the United States Army to move along.

She had two days to meet Aaron at the Texas border town of Stratford. Walking the plains in the heat of summer days and the cool nights would take sixty hours if she didn't stop, even once. The math didn't work, and she hoped he'd wait. If she didn't get there in time, more people would die. She had to get to Texas, and she had to move now.

Callie hadn't heard any noise from above in a while and decided it was safe to move out. The hatch hadn't sealed completely shut and there was just enough light to see outlines she recognized. She left the security of her computer and moved until she felt the cool, smooth cement wall. She knew the ladder was close by and felt along the wall until she gripped the cold aluminum rungs with both hands. She climbed toward the sliding exit, counting the steps as she rose. At the top, she listened for the rapid pop of gunfire. She listened for the brutal retort of the dying. She listened for the presence of the soldier's heavy boots. The only sound was the shallowness of her breath echoing off the door.

Callie pushed on the exit and ever so slowly slid the door ajar. The iron scent of blood, cooked flesh, and smoldering embers was like a boxer landing a punch to her nose. She stayed on her knees near the open bunker door and scanned the perimeter. Smoke flooded the air with a thin film of haze. The sun's rays poked through pockets of clean air and painted the tops of prairie grass with light. There didn't appear to be any sign of the United States. There were neither trucks nor troops. She listened closely and heard only silence. In that muted moment, the impossibility of her survival sunk in. Her head ached and she didn't want to move. She wanted to curl up and lie here until Aaron arrived. But that wasn't going to happen. If she was to help the Colorado Territory, she had to stand up and press on.

Callie rose from her knees and walked forward. Several corpses surrounded her. She searched their blank faces for life. Her heart beat faster and faster as if she could make up for those whose hearts stopped on an otherwise beautiful and ordinary morning.

She knelt by her sister's body and wept. As the tears rolled past her lips, the taste of salt reminded her of an organic truth— anger and resistance were as natural as the earth itself. As certain as the sight of Heather's blood, Callie was determined to make her anger felt by President Everett and all of his supporters.

A military response was the only solution to the problem of the Reclamation Movement, and she hoped to convince Aaron to use his. Texas had a cache of weapons as bountiful as their cache of oil. She'd persuade him that the Reclamation threatened the existence of Texas unless they retaliated for this action on Eads. Heather, victimized by this destruction, should be all the ammunition she needed to convince Aaron to act. Her life was worthy of swift, decisive action.

The sun shifted westward toward the horizon. The torrid heat of the late afternoon radiated throughout the plains as the leaves in a thin patch of trees winked in the hot wind. Just beyond the trees, a flag of the Colorado Territory adorned a leaning wooden flag pole. The ideals the flag stood for was tilted toward the edge of nonexistence. The Colorado Territory was a nation lying innocently in utero, waiting to take its first breath. Now labor had begun, and liberty lay in a breech position. Callie didn't want the Colorado Territory to die or put its mother at risk. Callie was this nation's mother and she was going to turn the baby around and fight for its right to be given a chance.

The site of the flag reminded her of Case. She knew the darkness of her thoughts would drive him away from her. Case was the one man she believed she could be with. His green eyes, coupled with his smile, were soft and sensitive. If she had wanted to, she could have invited more than conversation; but she wanted him to believe he was a strong man, one who could find the will to resist her feminine touch. She knew they would succeed as long as Case believed he was in control of his instinctual urges. So, she let him have it. And now she wished she hadn't. Maybe if they had kissed, even once, he'd have felt a love strong enough to fight instead of yielding to pacifism. Perhaps then he would have had the foresight to prevent the surrounding desolation.

If she could see him one more time, she would let their conversation end with extended eye contact and that familiar smile. She'd reach out and tenderly hold his hand. He'd laugh and playfully pretend to be coy. They'd kiss in an open, sun-lit field as their bodies became one, like their minds used to be. Callie's heart beat faster, but there was a hole within it, born from one part sorrow, one part frustration, and one part guilt. She squeezed her hands into a tight fist and inhaled.

The patter of a galloping horse took Callie away from her thoughts. The familiar pattern of hooves hitting the ground filled her ears with pleasantries, yet the cadence was frantic and off-beat. The horse crested a nearby hill and stopped at a patch of green land. The animal lowered its head and picked at the seeded tops of buffalo grass. He snorted and glanced around nervously with every bite. If Callie could catch the horse, she could tack it up and make it to Texas on time.

She approached, and the horse's ears and tail shot up. The apprehensive horse grunted, ready to bolt. Callie held her hand out. The horse stared at Callie with its wild eyes, sensing her motives. Callie reached out, but the horse took off and stopped twenty feet away.

"Shit," Callie said.

The sun seemed to move faster than usual as its light laced between low-hanging clouds. Occasional sage bushes dotted the rugged terrain. Chipmunks darted among the bushes seeking the solace of shade. Callie inched toward the horse. She just needed for him to get used to her until he stopped perceiving her as a threat.

From the distance, a loud whinny pierced the air and Callie recognized the whinny instantly. "Abby?" Callie said, responding to the call.

Another whinny and Abby appeared running toward the other horse. The large animals converged and stopped to confirm they knew each other with a gentle blow to each other's nose. Just seeing Abby alive gave Callie hope; somehow her trusted friend managed to escape.

"Abby," she said quietly. Callie understood horses, and she knew they never forget the ones that love them. "It's me, Callie," she said.

Abby's ears moved forward, a gesture of acceptance, and her tail swung in the breeze. When Abby lowered her head and picked at the stubby prairie grass with her teeth, Callie approached. While Abby remained calm, the other horse ran off at a gallop.

Callie took a step forward and extended her arm as an offering of peace to the animal. She noticed blood on Abby's back leg. A fairly fresh wound that likely needed some attention. Any injury to a leg could prove deadly to the horse.

Callie rubbed Abby's side as she examined the wound on the animal's stout rear leg. It didn't look great, and under normal circumstances, she would have treated the injury and allowed for a week of stall rest. But these weren't normal circumstances. Callie had to get to Texas, and Abby was her only chance of making it there on time.

"I'm gonna take care of you, girl," Callie said. "But I need your help first. Are you up for a ride?" Abby nickered at the sound of Callie's voice. Callie knew horses were loyal at heart and would do whatever was asked of them.

Callie's saddle and riding gear were in her barn and the only way to coax Abby back was to ride. She hadn't ridden bareback in some time, but Abby was gentle, and Callie knew the horse would tolerate her. They headed home.

The smell of smoke intensified as she got closer to her property. It smelled like a campfire, and Callie knew any fond memory the smell once brought about would be replaced with these unimaginable images. Reality is a greedy thief who steals the memories of youth and replaces them with the unpleasant memories of age. It comes with wisdom as a consolation prize, but wisdom is no more than a battle scar. Wisdom is a selfish mechanism in which we can say *I told you so*—when it ought to be an instrument for dreamers to say *Imagine if*.

Smoke emanated from the ashes that were once her house and her barn. There was nothing left. Her heart heaved with sorrow as she closed her eyes and prayed. She had selected this property on the day of her arrival. Because of Case's presence, Eads had become the epicenter of the freedom movement. She chose this spot because it was friendly to agriculture and the flat, open terrain made it so excavation wasn't a necessity.

She was welcomed and selected a plot on which to build. She built a small house with a bedroom and a barn for her horse. There was no need for any extravagances. Free will was her extravagance, and it was worth more than a formal dining room and vaulted ceilings.

Callie could take no more. She got back on Abby and walked toward Heather's barn. It was still standing, and for the first time today, there was a twinge of hope that maybe Henry was here. She dismounted and walked into the barn. Callie's skin pricked with the eerie sensation of standing in the shadow of her dead sister's ghost. She heard a sound and expected to see Henry, but instead, there was the only the hollow creak of a rusty gate swinging loosely in the soft breeze.

She found Heather's saddle, reins, and halter. She took them and secured them to Abby before entering Heather's small house for the last time. She searched for Henry, but the house was empty. On the nightstand was a silver locket. Callie picked it up and pried the locket open with her fingernails. On the left side was a picture of Henry. On the right was a picture of Callie, Heather, and Aaron when they were children. The picture represented a gleeful time before the Second Civil War when guns were made of fingers and figments of their imaginations, not possessions of protection and necessity. Tears found Callie's eyes once again and the locket jiggled in her shaky hands. This couldn't be happening. It didn't seem possible anyone else could have survived. Her sister was dead and her nephew was more than likely a victim as well, and for what? Somebody was going to pay. Callie had to get to Texas. She had to stop the bleeding of the people she loved.

Callie tucked the locket into her front pocket and returned to a patiently waiting Abby. She stroked Abby's black mane, jumped into the saddle, and started riding into town. Callie's stomach twisted at the idea of eating, but she knew eventually she would need something during the journey to Texas. She arrived at the central market which was normally well-stocked and organized, but now there were overturned tables and random produce strewn about the ground.

A flock of crows cawed loudly and fought each other for a

few kernels of corn. A turkey vulture strutted around like that of a starving and rabid vagabond with some kind of meat hanging from his long beak. Callie's head hung low as she scoured the scraps for something she could easily pack. She moved at the pace of a tortoise, and her exhausted legs wanted to quit. Her eyelids felt heavy and she wanted to indulge in the urge to close them. Maybe then she could dream her friends back to life, where they could share food and stories as if nothing happened.

The market was once a place where no money traded hands and nothing was ever bartered. It was not a place for material extravagance, but a place where people gathered to discuss life and philosophy. The only exchange that held any value was hugs for health and handshakes for happiness. The market represented more than food. The market was harmony, independence, and freedom. In short, the market was who they were.

None of that mattered now. As Callie scoured for any sustenance, her heart filled with emptiness and rage. How the United States could kill so ruthlessly was impossible to comprehend. She was going to stop them. If she could build bombs out of rotting food she would, and she would drop them over anyone who celebrated the flag of the United States.

Callie finally found some beef jerky, the perfect food to pack for her journey. She crudely stuffed the meat into her front pocket and ran back to Abby. She could bear the sights of what was no more. She mounted the mare and walked past the south side of Eads' small village. Any signs of life long ago evaporated into the dry air. Her body shuddered thinking about the scores of bodies left behind. The turkey vulture strutted about and gobbled. Callie's mind teased her with a waking nightmare as she envisioned the meat dangling from the vulture's crooked beak was flesh torn off the body of her friends.

Callie clenched her fist tight around Abby's reins and urged her into a trot. All Callie wanted was to get to Texas as fast as possible. She hoped like hell Aaron would give her what she wanted—weapons and troops. Maybe she'd need to offer something in exchange, though she had nothing to give.

As she passed the last living spaces of Eads, she wondered what became of Case. Had he met the same fate as her friends? Did he have something to do with the attack on Eads? Perhaps his attempt to negotiate for peace ended with a declaration of war instead. It could not be a coincidence that Case set out for negotiations and only two days later troops appeared at Eads' doorstep. She searched her soul. Even if Case were alive, he was as dead to her as Eads. His experiment with freedom in the Colorado Territory was gone. Eads will soon become the site in which the military prowess and extravaganza of the United States makes its triumphant return. What a coward Case was to not be here to observe it with his own eyes. She hoped he felt something sharp driven deep into his heart. She hoped in his final breath he heard the screams of his people calling out in agony. Yes, Case was dead to her, and because of him, so too was her sister.

She felt the locket burning against her leg. She slowed Abby to a walk and reached for the silver treasure. She observed the smiling face of Heather and knew she'd want revenge. She closed the locket, stuffed it back deep into her pocket and squeezed Abby's sides with her legs. The mare shifted directly to a canter. She had to get to Texas.

As Callie rode, the sun touched the horizon and long rays spread like a crown over a pink cloud. The wind slowed to a pleasant, cooling breeze and brought with it the fragrance of wildflowers and pine trees. On a normal evening, she may have basked with her friends in this beauty, as if an artist placed the sun there for the sole purpose of self-gratification.

Guilt cascaded through Callie's veins like an earth tremor. She was reminded just how irrelevant life sometimes was. The universe could care less that her friends were dead because if it did, the sun would have turned black and cast its fiery rays upon the evils of earth. Instead, it went about setting, pretending everything was okay.

The babbling of a brook made Callie realize how thirsty she was. She hadn't consumed even a drop in more than eight hours. Her mouth had turned into cotton, her spit tasted vile and suddenly getting water was of utmost importance. She pushed Abby forward and felt a limp in Abby's injured leg. At the brook, she could debride the wound, clean it with water and rest until morning.

Callie approached a daunting ravine. The brook lay at its bottom. There wasn't an easy path around as the scarred earth went for miles in either direction. She dismounted and peered into the steep ravine. One slip could mean the end for Abby and possibly serious injury for Callie. Yet the brook beckoned her down. The brook was their only source of water, and they desperately needed a drink.

"We can do this, girl," Callie said to her mare.

Callie steered Abby to the edge of trust between man and beast. Heading down a steep ravine on the back of a prey animal was akin to entering a strange universe in a foreign rocket ship, and her body shook with the g-forces of uncertainty. The fate of an entire country lay in the ability of an injured horse to maneuver into a deep rift.

She wondered if there were moments like this in the founding of the United States. Any singular moment left to fate could have altered history forever. What if George Washington's boat sunk into the icy tentacles of the Delaware River during the Revolution? Was there ever a moment that hinged on the success of a person and their animal? What of Paul Revere riding his steed, warning his fellow Americans of the Red Coats? What if his horse had become lame?

Callie held a clump of Abby's mane and encouraged her friend with a gentle squeeze of her legs. One simple misstep and it would all lie broken at the bottom. There was no room for mistakes. The mare shifted away, not wanting to go. Callie gently repositioned and tightened her legs around Abby's girth, urging the scared horse down.

The descent was slow and careful. Callie navigated around a thick cottonwood whose leaves seemed to cheer her on as they spun on their fragile stems in a faint breeze. Callie tried to harness nature's optimism, but Abby took a wrong step and slipped. The mare tumbled and flung Callie from her back. Callie hit the ground hard and her teeth clacked together as the wind was knocked out of her lungs. The horse skidded to an upside-down stop a few feet below.

Abby's four legs flared in the air until she finally managed to right herself. The horse looked around until she caught Callie's eye. Instead of running, Abby seemed to find faith in her rider. Callie caught her breath and allowed her pain to subside. She sat up and assessed her body. Somehow, nothing was broken. She stood and walked to Abby.

Abby seemed only stunned, but it would be impossible to know if anything was torn in her legs since she was already lame. The fall left both horse and rider close to the bottom of the ravine. Callie led Abby to the brook, making sure she'd be able to go on.

The brook wound its way through the ravine, its serene flow gently cascading over stones and pebbles. The final light of what felt like the longest day flickered on the water like a fading memory, though Callie knew the images she had borne witness to today would never fade. As Abby sunk her mouth into the river and drank, Callie slid her aching hands into the water and gently cupped the liquid to her parched lips. The cold water tasted of minerals and washed over her tongue with welcome relief.

Abby lifted her head and nickered, a sign of contentment. Callie stroked Abby's back and inspected the wound on her leg. The swelling was obvious, and the leg was hot to the touch. There was no doubt of an infection. Callie washed her hands in the brook and picked at the wound until she broke the scab. White pus and blood oozed from the hole. Abby shifted in discomfort but did not leave Callie's side. Callie squeezed the leg until the pus dissipated. Then she cupped water and washed the leg as well as she could. She tore fabric from her pants and tied it tight around the wound. She hoped rest would allow them both to move forward tomorrow.

In the final light of the day, Callie ate some jerky. As she glanced at the horizon, she noticed the subtle irony of power lines forming parallel horizontal streaks across the skyline. Electricity was lost long ago when the money from the United States government was cut off as a result of the treaty Case signed. She knew if she followed the lines northwest they would lead her to Denver, where the city rested in the darkness and emptiness of the times. Stadiums—once adorned with the names of powerful and rich companies—were now filled with dust escorted in by ordinary wind.

A smile found its way to Callie's face. She didn't miss those things at all. She remembered the day the lights went off in Eads. The subtle hum of electricity ended with the loud pop of an exploding transformer. She heard the cascading sound of appliances and lights going silent. That night, the community gathered outside, under the warm glow of the moon, lit candles, and promised the comfort of each other. At that moment, standing in a circle of light with her sister and new friends, Callie understood what love meant.

Every time she saw the power lines, she thought of them as false veins pumping electricity into houses filled with the inorganic glow of a television and computer screens. Those things seemed to her like viruses dimming the minds of its recipients with false light.

Mercifully, the sun set and the sky turned navy blue. The moon danced between clouds as Venus kept watch. The wind calmed and crickets chirped songs in unity. Abby found a spot to lay on and fell into a deep slumber. Callie bunked under a tree, her back against its sturdy trunk. Somehow, she managed to fade off to sleep.

Callie did not dream that night.

In the iridescent shades of early dawn, less than forty-eight hours after Callie vacated the underground bunker in Eads, she crested a grassy hill. The border city of Stratford, Texas glowed like a star; fueled by the richness of oil harvested from the Gulf of Mexico. She ground Abby to a halt at the top of the hill. The horse was struggling. She was tired and her limp was no better. She'd only a short more distance to go. Callie rubbed the soft, familiar leather reins between her fingers and moved toward the city lights.

Callie looked back at the northern horizon where the city lights were silently eaten by the anonymity of Colorado's trees. It had been only two days since Heather died, and Callie's heart beat with the emptiness of a rusted tin can. She looked toward Stratford and loosened the grip on the reins. The sudden urge to fill her loneliness with the comfort of a power button overwhelmed her inner core like the feeling of a smoker inhaling a cigarette after a long day without.

Her youth had been filled with light. She recalled playing hide and seek with her siblings until the incandescent streetlights flickered on, indicating it was time for dinner. Inside their large house, they would kick each other's legs at the table while their parents would dish out meat and mashed potatoes; comfort food at a time where everyone already felt comforted and loved.

Callie wanted to return to that feeling. Seeing the lights of Stratford reminded Callie how it was supposed to be. Life was about convenience and wealth. Life was about freedom, but freedom had to be protected by bombs and the largesse of government. The Stratford lights shone with the brightness of a wide-eyed teen, whose exciting future filled with the possibility of accumulation of wealth, had yet to unfurl. She wanted to deliver that normalcy to Colorado. The light beckoned her, and in an instant, her four years spent in the Colorado Territory was behind her as fast as the sun rose over Stratford.

Arrival felt like a victory, but there were still a lot of logistics to figure out. She thought of Aaron; the last time she saw him was at their father's funeral in Texas. Aaron never supported the Colorado Territory and believed its lack of governance was akin to the naive dreams of indelible youth. He felt people without the guidance of wise governance gravitated toward the most simplistic of animal emotions, those not based on logic or reason or morality, which ultimately lead to their self-destruction. This line of thinking has always been a central component of government royalty, and to admit otherwise would be the end of its power.

Callie was ready to accept the promise of protection over the fear of an unknown but certain death. Her naiveté died in the shadows of Eads, left on the soured battlefield to degrade into the bloodied soil and fertilize whatever generation occupied that land next.

The wind kicked up dust as she rode into the border town. They passed an old church and a large grain silo bearing the word STRATFORD in barn red letters. The exhausted mare was coated with sweat. She was completely lame and walked with an obvious limp. Callie dismounted, and the horse immediately lay down.

Abby closed her eyes and swooshed her tail. Her breathing became heavy and strained. Callie gently stroked Abby's neck and prayed. There was pain in Abby's tender eyes followed by peace. She blinked once and took her final breath. She was gone.

Tears flowed and the salt burned Callie's wind- and sun-reddened face. "You did your job, girl. You were my most loyal friend. You'll be the last victim," she said as she lowered her head onto Abby's motionless body. "I promise."

6

The heat of the day radiated against Case's open wounds—the rays of the sun were like razors on his flesh. The sharp, punchy smell of smoke emanating from holes in the ground caught Case's attention. The way the whispering smoke slithered low along the land reminded Case of a snake. It slyly rose and dissipated into the clouds above, taking with it the knowledge and memories of untold victims buried in the tragic catacombs below his feet. As he observed the destruction, there was no doubt in Case's mind that a bomb had been dropped on this place, no different than those used to flush out cowardly terrorists hiding in secret underground hideaways in Pakistan.

Case looked for any signs of active troop movement. To those faithful to the doctrine of the United States, the Colorado Territory was indeed filled with terrorists whose ideals threatened countries enslaved by money and power. The Colorado Territory destroyed the image that a pristine livelihood could only be brought about by the centralized authority of governmental power.

Case continued walking. The once-mighty giant windmills were broken and twisted as easily as used bread ties. Fallen with them was the idea that electricity would return to Colorado without the influence of outside money and government. Case knew that building a society would be slow, and these bombs only served to delay that process indefinitely. Case sighed and scrubbed his hands through his hair. He kicked at the dust on the ground.

As he scoured the warped metal, his mind replayed the image of Reed's body hitting the back wall of the holding cell. He had heard the bone-shattering thud and saw the oozing blood. His stomach soured and he fought back the urge to vomit. If he could just show the rest of the world the brutality of the United States, the images alone could be enough of a light to spark change. Alas, he had no camera—only mental images, and those were dark as he tried to make sense of it all.

Through the wisps of smoke, Case heard a noise. It was like that of an animal clawing at something. Then a soft, muted tone of what sounded like someone calling for help. He stopped and listened. Again, he heard it, "Please." The word sounded as if it were coming from where the bombs dropped.

"Help me," the desperate voice called.

Case stepped toward the voice and then stopped. In his hushed smoky surroundings, he thought he heard the sound of a vehicle. He listened intently but couldn't be certain. He couldn't be certain of anything anymore. He debated hiding but could never leave anyone for dead.

The beleaguered voice called again, "Please."

Case moved toward the voice. The bright sun, muted by the haze, made everything difficult to see. "Where are you?" Case called into the eerie smoke.

"Help." The voice was louder this time, perhaps fueled by the realization of nearby assistance.

Case turned, frantically looking for movement of any kind. "Please speak again," he said.

"Over here," the voice moaned.

As Case followed the voice, he stepped over deceased bodies, like macabre speedbumps, searching for the one that spoke.

"Over here," the frail voice was like thin glass.

As Case navigated closer to the place where the bomb had hit, the destruction became more evident. His legs sliced through the drifts of soft ash. The smell of soot and death plagued his nose yet allowed him to keep his mind grounded in the gravity of his search.

Among the hills of ash-white powder, the fresh vibrant red color of new blood stood out in contrast. He raced toward the sight and noticed subtle movement.

Case's body shook as he knelt next to the person. "I'm here," he said. "I'm gonna help you."

Eyelids peeled apart revealing big, blue, almond-shaped eyes. They were like a beam of bright light peering through the gray ash, and Case realized that he was looking into the eyes of a young woman. For a moment, her eyes held him captive by their mysterious beauty. Her gaze pierced his skin, found his inner being, and connected with him. It was beyond love at first sight. It was miraculous comfort, like someone he'd spent a lifetime with. Maybe it was the look of an ascended soul, or maybe it was the look of renewed hope; it struck Case that there was a reason he couldn't distinguish between the two.

Case dug in the loose soil and debris covering the girl. He should be able to drag her out now. He extended his hand. "Can you move your arm?" he asked.

She opened her right palm. It was broken and bleeding as if it had been scrubbed with rough sandpaper. She tried to extend her arm, but only managed inches. She kept her gaze fixed on his eyes.

Case looked at his palms, broken from his escape. The bleeding had ceased, but the pain of the fresh wounds still radiated from his hands and up his arms.

He showed her his hands and let her see his blood. She

nodded. "It's okay," she said. Her voice cracked, but she said the words with a steady confident tone. She had a strong will to survive.

Case gripped her wrist with his right hand and held her bloody, wet palm with his left. As their blood merged, he felt a sensation of understanding. This moment had played out before in a cosmic alternate universe captured in the stories written in the stars.

He gently pulled and her body shifted. As her torso slid forward, he noticed the unthinkable—she wore the fatigues of the United States Army. His heart sank as deep as that of a betrayed lover. He loosened his grip and her arm dropped to the ground. He looked at her face.

"Is something wrong?" she asked.

"Um," Case uttered. It was all his fuzzy, confused mind could manage. How could he allow her to live? After all, the country she represented bore the responsibility for the lives buried beneath the rubble.

Yes, she was complicit in taking the lives of innocent people. People who toiled with more purpose than money could have bought. With profits out of the picture, they were beholden to nothing. Their measure of success was not material but something esoteric, rarer than the purest gold. And while its harvest was possible for all mankind, this girl and her beautiful blue eyes stopped it dead.

Saving her equated to saving the very ideals he spent his life challenging. Case rose and turned his back. "You're from—" He couldn't say more.

"Yes," she said. "I'm from the United States."

He looked at her again. Her eyes shut, sealing her perfect blues behind the ashes caked on her eyelids. She looked like a crumbled statue. Crushing her skull would be no different than shattering the bust of a brutal dictator.

Case knew what he had to do, and he suspected the young woman knew what was coming. He searched the grounds for a large stone. He lifted its bulk in his arms and cradled it like a newborn. His back burned with a toxic mixture of passion for Colorado and hatred of how easily it could be turned to dust. The dead bodies around him represented years of work cowardly blown to bits in a second—no debate, no litigation.

Even with his back to her, he knew she had opened her eyes. Her stare bore into him, scorching him with guilt. Case lifted the stone over his head and spun around. He saw her open eyes—calm and contemplative. He held the weight of the stone as if it were the weight of his country. He steadied his quivering legs and took a deep breath.

If he killed her, he'd be no different than the enemy. He'd be no martyr—he'd be a murderer. He stood there for what seemed like a minute just holding the stone above his head. She never blinked. He let loose an animalistic scream and threw the stone away.

Case huffed as they silently looked at each other, searching each other's eyes for motives. He leaned over and reached for her open palm. She retracted her hand like a squirrel scurrying for the protection of its hole.

"I'm sorry," Case said. "I'm not going to hurt you. It's not who I am."

"I just want to get out of here alive," she said. "Our mission here is done. If you let me out, I will find my way home and not speak of our encounter."

She extended her hand. Case dragged her out from her entrapment. She sat upright; stunned, weak, and shaking. There were wounds on her scalp which were bleeding and Case wanted to make amends for his brutal thoughts. She was just a person in need of help.

Case bit his lower lip and could hardly bring himself to look the girl in her eyes. "Do you have water?" Case asked. "I'd like to clean your wounds."

She nodded toward a canteen strapped to her side, opposite her weapon. Case tore fabric from the bottom of his T-shirt, folded it inside out, and poured water on it. He kneeled next to her and gently wiped her face. As the water washed away the ash, it was like discovering beautiful art. Underneath the soot was the face of a woman, maybe twenty-one years of age.

Blood oozed from an open gash on her scalp. "Does it hurt?" he asked as he applied pressure to it.

"Yes," she said. She winced.

"Am I pressing too hard?" He would do anything to make her feel better.

"No," she said.

He maintained pressure on her wound and with his free hand, offered her the canteen. She reached for the water and her fingers brushed against his. When she touched him, his heart pounded rapidly. Within the surrounding haze of devastation was her internal light. Perhaps she was the reason he had survived at all.

She brought the canteen up to her dry lips, which parted gingerly as she took a sparing sip. Case noticed a fine pink hue returning to her face.

"You could use some too," she said, her voice tender and sweet. She flashed a brief smile as she handed him the water.

Case's knees wobbled as he took a sip from the canteen. The water was warm in his mouth and he could feel grit from his teeth. He wanted to spit it out, but he knew water was scarce. He squeezed his eyes shut as the water burned his parched throat.

"It's okay," she said. "Please take a generous sip. I can tell you need it more than me."

Case obliged and consumed a healthy swallow. His body absorbed the fluid almost immediately and the sustained tension in his shoulders eased. He handed the canteen back to her. "Thank you," he said, as they made brief eye contact.

The sun hid behind a large white cloud, offering welcome shade as the two recovered within the obscurity of the smoky fog. The few remaining windmills stood guard; their slender arms still from the lack of wind. An unnerving silence surrounded them; it was evident there were no other survivors. On the horizon, the promise of clear green fields beckoned. It was the United States which lay eastward, beyond the border, that Case worried about the most.

"What's your name?" Case asked, with the reticence of a teenage boy asking for a girl's phone number.

Full color returned to her face, pink and lively. "Renna," she answered. Case could almost feel her energy returning and she seemed to share it with him. "What's yours?"

"My name is—" he hesitated for a moment. His was a name that came with recognition. "Case," he finished.

She squinted. He was as sure as the blue of her eyes that she knew the name. How could she not?

"You didn't kill me," she said. "My platoon just eliminated this place from the map, and you let me live. Why?"

Case shifted uncomfortably. "I guess I just couldn't," he replied. "But you're the one with the weapon." He gestured toward her gun.

"I know. You spared my life. I owe you the same bit of respect."

"Well, that's good," Case chuckled. "So now that we have that out of the way, what's next?"

"I'd like to move out of this fucking smoke," Renna said with a tepid smile and a cute breathy laugh.

"So would I," Case said, his heart fluttering at her humor.

He rose and took her by the hands. She was unstable for a moment but managed to find the strength to stand steadily. Case let her hands go and pointed to a clearing east of the rubble. They walked side by side in that direction. There was an electricity running through his veins he'd never experienced before, and he wondered if she sensed a connection between them as well.

Clean, fresh air filled Case's lungs in refreshing abundance; so much so that he could almost taste a sweetness in the air reminiscent of honey. Renna's heavy army gear clanked in the rhythmic cadence of her sure gait. As she walked, her uniform cast off dust like she was shedding the skin of an illicit past. Case snuck occasional glances at Renna's figure, and despite the bulk of her uniform, it managed to complement her slender, fit shape. She was as physically strong as her mind seemed to be.

Renna stopped, found her canteen, and took a generous slug. She handed the canteen to Case. He gulped some down with ease this time. His body was already healing.

As they rested a moment, Renna asked, "You said your name was Case. Are you Case Tappan?"

"Yes," he said.

"Our intel had you in Eads," Renna said. "But then our mission switched to this place. They must have known you were here."

Case didn't respond. A robust drop of sweat ran down his forehead. He wiped it off with his bare arm.

Renna exhaled loudly and fidgeted with her canteen. "You know..."

"What?" Case said.

She rocked back and forth and looked away, searching for words. "You would have been justified," she said.

"What do you mean justified?" Case asked.

"Killing me with that stone. I saw the look in your eyes the moment before you changed your mind. The look of—"

Case waved his hand. He did not need her to describe his look to him. Holding that stone was already the darkest moment of his life. He knew for certain now he'd rather wield the pen of diplomacy than a weapon of any kind. Ever.

"We are, after all, at war," she finished.

"Are we?" Case asked.

"Yes," she responded.

The simplicity of her response left a pit in Case's stomach. "It's your war then. Not mine."

Renna took in her surroundings, in the way of a soldier in survival mode. "But it is yours," she insisted. "You're the reason." She appeared about six years his junior. Four years ago, while he inked treaties, she would have been in high school, contemplating her involvement in the civil war with Texas.

"The reason for what?"

"There is a lot of suffering in America," she said. "The cost of food is so high that there are hours-long lines at the stores for bread and milk. President Everett says it's because you took our land. There are not enough jobs for everyone, and more than half the population is on welfare. He said that since you took our land the jobs went with it. The price of gas is outrageous, and Everett said without this land, the oil shortage will continue. Violent crime is higher than ever. People have been mugged, beaten, and killed for luxuries like hamburger. Everett said since you took a lot of our farmland, there isn't enough room to keep cattle. Everyone is on edge. You can't even look at someone without stoking fear. You can't count on a handshake to having any weight behind it. And perhaps most importantly, since there is no trust, I've noticed there is no love anymore." As Renna talked, her arms flailed about.

"Am I to blame for that as well? The lack of love?" Case asked.

"Everett says so," Renna answered.

"I know what Everett thinks," Case retorted. "Is that what you believe?"

Renna's rapid body movements stopped. She crossed her arms. "It's what we're told."

Case cringed at the notion of being told what to believe. Manipulation of fragile, youthful minds was perhaps the most heinous of the war crimes committed by the United States. "I understand what you're told," he pressed. "But is that what you believe?"

She glanced down. "No," she answered.

A subtle breeze caused the prairie grasses to rustle and ebb like a vast golden ocean. The flag of the Colorado Territory fluttered on a nearby pole.

Case watched the flag intently. "Do you know where you are?" Case asked.

"Most certainly," she responded. "I was assigned ground response during the raid of the Colorado Territory. I suspect I've been left for dead."

"That's not what I mean."

She tilted her head. "What do you mean then?"

Case pointed to the flag. "I made that image," he said. "Do you know what that flag represents?"

She observed the flag for a moment.

"You say that I would have been justified," he said. "Bashing that stone into your skull."

"I believe that," she responded. "These are the rules of war."

"The rules of war," he chuckled. "Had I killed you, it would have changed everything I believe in. Had I killed you, the image on that flag would have been meaningless."

"So where am I then?" she asked boldly. It was not a question of uncertainty or confusion. It was a question formed of profoundly rapid and adept understanding.

Case smiled. "You are with me," he said. "We are two individuals, here together. That flag means I have an obligation to respect you as a person. It means I have an obligation to promote unity no matter where we stand."

The breeze cascaded through Renna's blonde hair. A few strands blew gently across her face, and she brushed them away. "I guess that's where I am then," she said. She inhaled deeply and her chest rose as if in defiance of the uniform she wore.

"I really don't think my platoon would have returned for me," she said, her mood suddenly changed. The realization of how close she had come to dying was settling in.

A tear welled in her eye and cascaded down her blushing cheek. Within that tear lay the images of war's grotesque hostility and obscene magnitude of hatred.

"We don't even have to see it anymore," She said fighting off more tears.

"See what?" Case asked. He reached out and gently rubbed her back.

"The carnage of war. It's not shown in movies anymore, it's not critiqued by the media. War's blood is muted and scrubbed. It's like video game violence. It's just not real."

"Now you see how very real it is, don't you?" Case asked gently.

Renna nodded. "The bodies were all around me. The screams were unbearable. I saw a woman push her intestines back into a hole in her stomach before collapsing and dying. Then I was buried and couldn't see. I remember thinking, being blind is better. I don't want to see this shit anymore." Renna's sobs intensified. "I can't even—"

Case held her shoulders and looked deeply into her wet, blue eyes. "Tell me, Renna. If they did see it, would it end the war?"

Case waited as Renna sobbed for a moment longer. "I would hope so," she answered, with a quiet smile.

"As do I," Case replied. "Which is why I need to get to the border."

Renna's lips morphed into a frown. "To the border?" she said. "You know they'll put you in prison."

"I know," he sighed.

"But you can't. We just met," Renna said.

"I think there will be lots of time to get to know each other. But for now, I need your help."

"My help? How?"

Case held out his wrists and pointed to her gun. "I'm your prisoner," he said. "Take me to your leader."

"Case. I can't—"

"Yes, you can," Case said. "If we are at war, you have an obligation to your flag. I don't want anything bad to happen to you. We go to the border."

7

Texas. The sun rose and cast a pink hue over the small sleepy town of Stratford. Callie absorbed the welcoming warmth of the morning sun on her skin, as memories of her journey here faded. She was finally home again, and the events of the last few days were buried by the familiar sights and sounds of Texas. The hustle and bustle of commerce lined Main Street with an old fashioned vibe. The faint glow of an orange "Open" sign dressed the window of an ice cream parlor; a helix of colored stripes on a pole signified a barbershop. The incredible smells from a nearby diner made her stomach ache for food. The type of food she remembered fondly before the Colorado Territory even existed, greasy and deep-fried. The nostalgia was overwhelming, and an inexplicable sensation of comfort walked into the open door of her soul.

As she searched for the corner of Canterberry and Daliah Streets in hopes that Aaron would be there, she reminded herself this feeling of comfort came at a steep cost. After Texas separated from the Union, it owned all the oil operations in the

Gulf. Like the United States, once central authorities in Texas manage the concentration of wealth, life becomes like a carnival graviton. Balance is maintained by centrally located operators who control the speed and monitor passengers from a focal point. When the floor drops, only the government can stop the ride.

Callie wound through the maze of town blocks until she stumbled to Canterberry and Daliah. There was no limo waiting for her. The citizens of Stratford had begun their daily routines, and the buzz of life surrounded her. She stood on the street corner and paced like a child waiting for a school bus for the first time. She noticed the number of times the streetlight turned from red to green and even started calculating the minutes she has been waiting—at least thirty by now. She glanced at her ragged clothes. Her pants were torn from the tourniquet she made for her beloved Abby. Her skin crawled with the sensation of surly judgmental eyes upon her. As people walked by, she looked down so as not to draw attention to herself.

The motion of a black car on the street stole Callie's attention. It was only a black sedan with dark tinted windows. Still, Aaron hadn't said it would be a limo. It must have waited through at least two light cycles by now. She ran toward it just as the car pulled slowly away.

She crossed the street waving her hands at the car. "Wait," she called, but the car drove away.

She reached the other side of the street to the stares of several people. One such person was a large man with a shaved head. The vibrancy of muscles evident under a tight black suit gave the appearance of both danger and security. Her hands were clammy, and she walked faster. The man followed her.

"Hey," the man called.

Callie turned. "Can I help you?" Callie asked.

The man stopped and smiled at her. "Does it look like I need help, Callie?" He said, his husky voice echoed off the brick walls of buildings, but his tone was friendly.

"Do I know you?" She said in a heavy breath.

"I'm not gonna hurt you," the man said. "I was sent to come and get you."

Callie's body relaxed and her mental wall broke down. "Sent by Aaron?"

The man nodded and then spoke into a small mobile device. "I've got her," he said. He looked at Callie. "Yes. I was sent by your brother Aaron. You may not know me, but I've certainly been expecting you."

The black sedan returned, and the man opened the back door. "This is for you, too," he said.

Callie stood next to the door. This was her last chance to change her mind. Once she got in, she'd be on her way to Aaron. She reached for the locket in her pocket and rubbed it between her thumb and pointer finger.

"Go ahead," the man said. "It'll be okay."

Callie nodded and ducked into the car. The luxurious smell of leather struck her nose. The driver turned and faced Callie. He was dressed in a suit, his shoulders were broad, and his voice was pleasant and welcoming. "It's about an hour to Amarillo," he said with a smile. "I'm taking you directly to Aaron Stanton."

"That's perfect," Callie said as they pulled away. A cold beverage lay in wait in the armrest. She took a sip and let the coolness coat the back of her throat. Within moments the beverage was gone.

The car moved fast along a wide-open highway. They traveled at a high rate of speed. There were no posted speed limits and Callie wondered if it were some kind of government superhighway funded by all that exuberant oil cash.

As they cruised along uninterrupted, the landscape blazed by. The terrain was familiar, yet there were fewer people. Callie whizzed by ghost town after ghost town. Towns, she recalled, that were once vibrant places to live.

"Where is everybody?" she asked the driver. "This stretch is usually busy, isn't it?"

The driver's face appeared in the rearview mirror. His brown eyes made eye contact and then returned to the road. "Not so much anymore," he said. "Everyone who stayed after the civil war lives in the big cities now, Houston and Dallas mostly. A lot of people left Texas, most of 'em went to live in the United States. I guess they preferred them to us."

"Really?" Callie said. "That's interesting."

"Good riddance, I say. If you aren't with us, then you're our enemy," the driver responded.

Callie nodded and watched as they passed one quiet little town after another. The car slowed to maybe seventy-five miles per hour as it exited the highway. Through the tinted window lay the city of Amarillo. The sign along the exit in all caps read, REMEMBER AMARILLO. It was here, within these city limits, at 7:51 p.m. ten years ago, when the United States Army fired upon citizens staging a protest about federal government overreach. The protest had been brought about by a federal ban and seizure of weapons, and the elimination of the word God from any public record. These were definitely two things the people in Texas could not let go of. The crowd had grown to the thousands and tensions surged when a counter-protest formed. The United States sent in the military to control potential violence, but when tensions boiled over, the United States took a side and proceeded to mow down a countless number of government protesters. At that moment, everything had changed.

Callie and Aaron had lived within the city limits and were forced into lockdown. While she couldn't bring herself to watch out the window then, she heard the sound of machine guns, much like the ones she had heard in Eads, firing bullets. It seemed no matter where she lived, her perspective was shaped by the exit wounds left by the bullets of a government she was supposed to trust.

Civil war broke out only two days later as the people of Texas sought revenge before their guns were confiscated. A citizen militia, which included Aaron, opened fire at a municipal building in Amarillo, taking the lives of nine US officials. Callie wanted nothing to do with it, and at Aaron's suggestion, she and Heather left everything and everybody and moved to Colorado. It is there Callie met Case and joined him in the successful effort to sign a peace treaty with the United States.

If only she had the foresight to see that moving to Colorado solved nothing. The idea of a truly free society had fallen short and it was four years of her life she wanted back. She had been concerned about violence when talk of the Reclamation began, but she trusted Case. That trust had cost her the life of her sister. Suddenly, Case became nothing more to her than an obsessive cult leader. Regret swam in her stomach like a virus. She clutched her drink tight and pressed her feet against the floor of the car. It was beyond time to reconnect with Aaron and more than ever she was ready to return home.

8

Aaron sat upright in his office chair and scrolled through US newsfeeds looking for any information he could find about the attack on Eads. There was nothing. The mission was not intended for public consumption. There had to have been something picked up on radar. He searched his contacts and dialed Henderson, his Director of Military Intelligence and Surveillance.

"We detected nothing in Eads," Henderson said. "You said the army was likely on foot?"

"I believe this to be the situation," Aaron answered.

"That would be almost impossible to detect with our system. It looks for larger activity. Or if we happen to catch military chatter on our radio frequency monitors. But that is getting harder to read with the advanced technology in encryption."

"So, you really can only detect bombs?" Aaron asked.

"Yes. Bombs and jets," Henderson said. "Funny you mention this because we did detect something due east of there within the past few hours. We were just able to confirm that our radar picked up the presence of possible military jets near the Kansas border. We also detected seismic activity in the same location. It has the signature of a bomb. There has been chatter surrounding the death of Case Tappan as well."

"Case Tappan?" Aaron said, "I assumed he died in Eads."

"Pardon?" Henderson asked.

"Never mind. Thank you, Henderson. Keep me posted with any new developments," Aaron said and ended the call.

Maybe the attack wasn't personal. Maybe the United States had been pursuing Case all along. After all, Case was the face of the Colorado Territory. Callie hadn't mentioned him on the call, so it served to reason he was not in Eads at the time of the attack. The US media wouldn't be privy to the situation until the army captured or killed the face of the movement.

President Everett's message to the United States media would have to be good news, not near misses. It was sickening to think that had both of his sisters died, he would never have even known. The tension in his shoulders reached a crescendo and blood coursed fiercely through his veins. His fingers tapped a staccato beat on his desk.

He picked up his phone and made another call. "How rapidly could we prepare troops?" he asked Sergeant Levi Miller.

"We could have troops prepared to defend us instantly, sir." Levi Miller responded.

"How about to engage?" Aaron asked.

"To engage, sir?" Sergeant Miller asked, surprised. "With whom?"

"I am just getting a sense of preparedness," Aaron said. "With anyone." Even though the air conditioner pumped cool air into his office, Aaron wiped the sweat from his brow.

"That depends, sir," Sergeant Miller said. "If you are talking about the United States, we are prepared to engage on command, but that does not mean we have the sophistication to defeat them in battle. We are still behind in advanced weaponry."

Aaron ran his fingers through his hair. The Texas Territory

had existed for only four years and the United States for three hundred. During the Second Civil War, the mood in the United States was that of negotiation, not continued battle. With Everett in command, all that changed. Every last dime in the US budget was earmarked for the Reclamation. Aaron realized Texas would have to increase spending significantly to deal with this threat. But for now, he had to deal with the situation at hand.

He reached for the Bible on his desk and tapped on its black cover. It reminded him that the good Lord protected Texas because the success of Texas was in God's plans. No army was big enough to defeat God's will.

"Is there something I should be aware of, sir?" Sergeant Miller asked.

Aaron sat back in his chair. A tangible stillness enveloped the room. "I don't know," Aaron answered. "It's nothing I can discuss at the moment."

"Yes, sir," Miller said.

Aaron shifted in his chair and it creaked as he adjusted his seat. "Are the men prepared?" Aaron asked.

"Pardon, sir?" Sergeant Miller said. "Didn't you just ask me that?"

"I mean are the men mentally prepared?" Aaron pressed. "Are they ready to die?"

"These are honorable men," Miller responded. "They are willing to die for their country."

"That's not what I asked," Aaron insisted.

"Sir?"

"Are they ready to die?" Aaron reiterated.

"I don't think any of them are ready to die," Sergeant Miller said. The soft tone in his voice suggested he was disappointed he couldn't answer to the affirmative. Aaron knew Miller was admirable and for him to admit a weakness was obviously difficult.

Aaron knew that was the difference. The United States

recruited people and turned them into machines. The government stripped recruits down to their very core, shaved their heads, put them in uniforms, and controlled their behavior. This is done not in hopes of helping them discover who they really are, but to build a corps of living souls who are not only ready to die but expect it. The amount of psychology used to develop the American soldier is comparable to none. When that power is used to promote good, it is incredible, but when it is used for revenge, as it was now, it's a gift straight from hell.

"Tell me, Sergeant," Aaron said. "How do we get them ready?"

"I don't know," Sergeant Miller said. "I suppose they have to become numb to the violence. Once a person has seen enough violence, they are capable of tuning it out. Kind of like a defense mechanism. Nature's way of suspending one's disbelief, I guess. Sir, is there something you wish to tell me about?"

"The Reclamation has begun, and it's getting close to Texas," Aaron said. "I need you and your men to be ready."

There was a long pause. Aaron heard only Miller's breathing. "I'm ready," he said. "Every great nation has to fight to survive, and God willing I will be remembered as a hero who died with honor. That's all I could ask for."

"Thank you, Sergeant," Aaron said. "We will only engage in just action. Keep alert and may God bless you."

"Will do, sir," Miller said. "Is there anything else?"

"No," Aaron replied. "That's all." Aaron ended the call.

Aaron rested his hands on his desk and thought of Heather. The last time he saw her sweet face was four years ago. Tears welled up in his eyes and he fought them off. He needed to harness this energy and find a way to make Heather's death mean something. There was only one way. He picked up his phone again and dialed Russo.

"Mr. Stanton," Russo said. His salutation sounded rapid and impatient.

"Mr. President. There has been a second attack within

the Colorado Territory. This one near the Kansas border. It is possible that Case Tappan was killed in the attack. I do believe the US is after its titular leader."

"What do you suppose will happen next?" Russo asked.

Aaron scratched his chin. "The news of Case's death will be made public and this will embolden the United States to continue their reclamation efforts. I don't think we should allow this," Aaron answered.

"What are you suggesting?"

Aaron glanced around the room, stopping again at his Medal of Courage. "I am suggesting military intervention at the border."

"On what grounds?"

"Humanitarian crisis."

"What is the potential impact on Texas of such an intervention?" Russo asked.

"Military casualties," Aaron answered.

"Anything else?" Russo asked.

"I suppose there is a risk of escalation," Aaron said.

"Aaron," Russo said. "Of course, there is a risk of escalation. I should not have to pry that out of you."

"Sir, I—" Aaron started.

"I am not in the mood for war," Russo interrupted. "Nor am I willing to risk the lives of Texans for land that is not even ours. You are reacting emotionally over this and I am concerned for you."

"Concerned, sir?"

"Yes. I have never before thought of your judgment as clouded. I cannot have that. I am not certain you are the correct point of contact for advisement concerning this matter."

"Are you firing me, sir?" Aaron asked. His jaw clenched with the fear of losing his position within the Texas Territory for which he'd taken an oath to protect and serve.

"No," Russo said. "I am recusing you from this situation."

"You can't do that. I must remain actively involved. This is a serious threat. What do I have to say to convince you?"

"Aaron, why don't you take some time off? It's been four years since you've even taken a vacation. Take some time off so you can properly mourn the loss of your sister."

Aaron gritted his teeth. Vacation at a time like this was absurd. Yes, he was emotional, but he could set his sister's death aside for the sake of the country. Why couldn't Russo see this? It was the first time in his career he had been overridden by Russo. Disagreements at this level never ended well. Someone was going to be wrong, and it wasn't going to be Aaron.

"This is no time for vacation," Aaron said. "We must address this situation."

"Your concern has been noted, but I am no longer asking. Take a week off. That's an order."

"With all due respect, sir. A week could wipe out all of Colorado. We must act," Aaron insisted.

"Sometimes inaction is the best action. There is nothing to be done at this point."

The phone was heavy in Aaron's hands. He knew there was a limit to Russo's patience. If Aaron was removed from office, he'd be utterly powerless, and he knew he must say the right thing, even if it was a lie. "Very well. I will take some time off, but I will be receiving updates. If anything changes, I will inform you." The lie lingered on his tongue like the taste of a bitter apple.

"You've made a wise decision," Russo said. "Be well."

The call ended.

Aaron pursed his lips and glanced around the room. He stopped at the Washington Post article again. The boy in that picture was willing to disobey orders. The man sitting on his chair was the same person. He wasn't going to head to the beach and cry. He was going to act even if Russo wasn't.

Aaron's phone rang. It was Lindsey Nichols, the colleague in charge of Callie's retrieval.

"Yes," Aaron said.

"Mr. Stanton. We've retrieved Callie."

Aaron breathed a sigh of relief. Callie was safe. As much as he wanted to grieve with her, there was work to be done.

"Very well," Aaron said. "I am on my way to Amarillo."

9

Callie's car slowed to a stop somewhere in Amarillo. The stocky driver got out and opened Callie's door. Humidity staggered into the car and settled uncomfortably on her skin. Outside, a dark thundercloud formed overhead. As she stepped away from the car, a strong wind blew across her face. Her brother exited a second sedan and faced Callie. He wore a perfectly tailored black suit with a straight-legged pant, a white shirt, and a red tie. A pin with the flag of Texas worn on his lapel embellished his otherwise staid apparel. His static visage showed no emotion. His lips formed a straight line across his face indicating words were not going to be easy to come by or even friendly. His brown eyes remained steady and fixed directly at Callie, suggesting a seriousness surrounding their meeting. He dropped a pair of mirrored sunglasses over them, shielding whatever intentions his eyes may have already exposed.

Aaron extended his hand, as he might with any other dignitary from a foreign land. She shook it. His grip was tight and rushed; he was ready to get out of this location. He escorted

Callie into his vehicle and sat down in the back seat next to her. The car pushed ahead.

Aaron's face was skeptical and unforgiving. Clearly, a job like his hardened the soft heart of her formerly caring brother.

"Where are we going?" she asked.

"I'm taking you home," he answered. Aaron urged the driver to move faster. Callie wondered if all this was a mistake. What chance did she have to convince her brother of anything?

"Aaron," she started, but his cell phone interrupted her.

Aaron looked at the screen. "I've got to take this," he said, and turned his body in such a way that whomever the caller was, they were more important than his own sister facing a crisis like no other time in her life.

Was there no forgiveness in his heart? Was she to blame for Heather's loss? She knew she wasn't. Heather had gone to Colorado on her own accord. Goddamn it; Callie couldn't help but think Heather would be alive if only she had listened to her big brother.

Aaron's call ended. He sat back in his seat, lifted his sunglasses to the top of his head, and stroked his chin. Perhaps he was thinking of dropping her off in a dark alley somewhere just to be taught a lesson.

"Aaron," she whispered.

He looked at her and sighed but seemed open to whatever Callie had to say next. She thought maybe if she appealed to his soft side it would ease the tension that radiated tightly through her body. "Do you remember Jaxson Henly?"

Aaron furrowed his brow. "Jaxson Henly?" he said. "That boyfriend of yours that hit you?"

Callie nodded. "Yes."

"What about him?"

"Do you remember what you did to him?" she asked.

She pictured Jaxson's large hand coming down across her face, busting her lip. She could almost taste the blood swirling on her tongue.

"I beat the shit out of him," Aaron said.

"That's right," Callie said.

"Right outside his own damn house," Aaron said; his eyes distant as if imagining swinging his fists at Jaxson's unsuspecting face. Callie had been there, watching from within the security of the passenger seat of Aaron's old Ford pickup. She could even see Aaron's silver crucifix dangling from the rearview mirror. There was a shotgun strapped to a rack on the ceiling of the pickup. It was there if she needed it.

"Did you know I dated him for two more months after that?" Callie said.

"I know," Aaron said. "I never understood why though."

"I was just a stupid kid," Callie said. "I didn't know trouble if it smacked me in the face. And it did, quite literally."

Aaron nodded. "Callie, what's this got to do with anything?"

"Sometimes I'm still that kid," she said. Callie sighed, the tension in her body eased. The words needed to come out. "I know I've fucked up. But the Aaron who beat up Jaxson, that's the brother I need right now."

The look on Aaron's face reminded Callie of their childhood. "After you called, I wasn't certain I'd see you ever again," Aaron said. "I'm still in shock over the news of Heather and Henry."

Callie nodded and lowered her head, half expecting him to pile onto the guilt she already felt. But he didn't. The air seemed thick and somber on Callie's skin.

"Do you still believe in God?" he asked. Goosebumps appeared on Callie's arms. She supposed it was an appropriate question given the topic. She couldn't answer and looked away.

"Did you pray, Callie? When you watched Heather die, did you say a prayer?" he asked.

Tears formed in Callie's eyes, for she knew she hadn't prayed. In her heart, it was God she blamed. She was just as much a victim as Heather. "Don't do this," Callie said. "Who's praying for me? When was the last time you bowed your head and asked God to watch over me?"

Aaron looked out the window. "I pray for you every day," he said. "Maybe that's why God saved you—to bring us together again. To unite us so we can make Heather's death mean something."

"Maybe," Callie answered. She was raised to accept God's will.

"God unites the strong," Aaron said. "We fight together in the advancement of His will. Those secure with faith don't lose, Callie. And I don't lose. God help us if I did. It's probably something you forgot living in Colorado."

"What do you mean?"

"You abandoned your faith," Aaron said. "Why did you stay there, Callie? You never really explained it. I need to understand you if I am to help you."

"I stayed because I was scared of war. It seemed wrong," Callie said. "I was young, and I didn't get that Texas was fighting for the things I believed in, because I didn't know what I believed. Colorado was an easy escape."

"I warned you of this during the Amarillo War. No country can survive with pacifism at its roots. Yet you believed in it," Aaron said. "You believed in the concept of the Colorado Territory, didn't you?"

"I did," Callie said, still drying the tears brought about by the thoughts of her sister. She sighed deeply. "Look where it got me. It took Heather away from me. Away from us. I just—"

"The Colorado Territory is a barren, Godless land," Aaron said. "Maybe that's why all this happened."

Callie hadn't considered that notion. Perhaps Aaron was right. "Maybe," she said. "Or maybe it's because we had no way to protect ourselves."

"Do you still believe in it?" Aaron asked.

Callie looked out the window. The landscaped rushed by faster than her teary eyes could focus. She folded her hands into her lap and looked at Arron. "I've come to believe that Case was wrong. He was stubborn, but I was in love with him."

"Kind of like you were in love with Jaxson," Aaron said.

"Yeah," Callie replied. "Kind of like that, I guess. But I learned from that. I am stronger now. My eyes have seen too much. I won't be the kid in the front seat of your truck watching you kick the shit out of Jaxson on my behalf. This is why I am here. I am not going to take this bullshit anymore." She wiped the final tears from her face. She didn't feel like crying anymore; it served no purpose.

It was at that moment Callie remembered the silver locket tucked deep in her pocket. She reached in, took it out, and opened it up. "I found this at Heather's place after the attack," she showed Aaron the picture of the three of them together. This time it was Aaron who seemed to fight off tears. "I was a kid in this picture, just like you were. I want that feeling back."

She handed the locket to Aaron. He looked at it for some time and then folded it into his palm. He hunched over in the car seat, hung his sunglasses on his shirt pocket, and closed his eyes. When he looked up, his disapproving look had softened. Callie recognized it. It was the look only a protective older brother could give his younger sister. It was her favorite look of his because she knew she had his full attention. "Let's talk inside," he said. "We're home now."

The black sedan pulled off the road and onto a meandering driveway of what appeared to be a Texas-style ranch. They passed horses and cattle grazing in lush fields. The driver parked the car and let the siblings out. Overhead, a plump storm cloud was ready to unleash its pent-up fury. As thunder reverberated, a heavy drop of rain hit Callie's arm with a hearty thud. She covered her head and followed Aaron inside as the rain unloaded on the sunbaked ground.

They entered Aaron's house. Trophy heads lined the walls of the grand entrance. Their glass eyes seemed to stare at Callie with disparaging looks. Large fans hung from thick oak beams on the high vaulted ceilings, circulating refreshing cool air. The west-facing wall was comprised of nothing but windows allowing for a view of the sunset. Built-in shelves along the east wall contained finely crafted models of slender oil derricks. On every wall, pictures of massive Gulf Ocean oil rigs hung with perfect balance. It was clear to Callie what priorities Aaron valued most. Oil was his family now—his lifeblood, his security, his God. There was no doubt he'd protect it with all of the power granted to him through the state.

A man entered the room, holding a towel, soap, and new clothing. "Would you care to clean up?" he asked Callie.

She nodded, and the man escorted Callie to the entrance of a private bathroom. She locked the door behind her and turned on the shower. Warm water poured through her soul. How she missed the simplicity and ease of indoor plumbing. It was a life she could get used to again. It was a life she now regretted leaving in the first place.

The clothes provided were that of business attire—a white shirt, navy pants, and a matching jacket. The clothes hugged her body with a sense of respect. She ran her fingers through her refreshed black hair. Color returned to her face and her brown eyes beamed back at her in the mirror. She hadn't taken the time to appreciate her appearance in four years. There always seemed something more important to do, but today she allowed herself the indulgence.

Upon her return to the great room, Aaron was alone, seated in an overly large leather chair. He had changed into a business casual look. The tie and jacket were gone and so too were his mirrored sunglasses. An arrangement of aromatic fruits, crackers and cheeses was freely available. The sweet smell of fresh fruit filled her with cautious delight. Callie placed a respectful amount on her plate even though she could have consumed the entire serving dish.

Aaron motioned for her to sit in the matching chair across from him. She sat and her arms quivered as her nerves built up anticipation.

"Okay," Aaron said. "I pulled some strings and was able to

secure asylum for you. I want you to know, you are safe here."

"Asylum?" Callie said with a smile. "I guess you do have some power around here."

Aaron laughed. "Well, if you consider direct access to President Russo power, then I guess so."

The smile disappeared from Callie's face. Maybe it was inspired by her new clothes, but Callie wanted to get down to business. "That's good, Aaron. Is Russo ready to stop the United States?" Callie asked. "I am. I'm ready to pull the gun off the rack of your old pickup truck and use it."

Aaron shifted in his seat. "Let's just get you reacquainted with life in Texas first," he said.

"But the Reclamation has begun, Aaron. The United States is taking back the land," Callie responded.

"I am aware," Aaron said. "I can assure you Texas is not in danger. I can probably get you some kind of position within the government, for starters."

Callie squeezed the armrest with both hands and shook her head. "A job? You're offering me a job? Aaron, we've got to do something."

"Do something? You are safe now, isn't that what you wanted?" Aaron sat back in his chair, took a sip of water and crossed his legs. "Perhaps you should consider yourself fortunate just to be here."

Callie's body trembled and she resisted the urge to scream at him. "People are being murdered. It's not their fault. We can't just watch." Callie said, sitting upright in her seat, eyes fixed on her brother like unrelenting lasers. "You said yourself that Heather's death meant something. We can do that by salvaging the Colorado Territory. Not by giving me a job."

Aaron sifted in his seat. "It isn't worth saving," Aaron said, straight-faced and matter-of-factly.

The words sunk Callie's heart, but gravity is reality. "You don't see it do you, Aaron?"

"See what?"

"You seem to think the Reclamation is only about the Colorado Territory," Callie said. "When the US takes Colorado and reclaims the resources, they will become emboldened. Who do you think they'll come for next? Do you think President Everett gives a damn about your sovereignty? Do you think he takes the Colorado Territory and just stops? Colorado has nothing; Texas on the other hand—" she paused briefly. "Texas has everything. If it's money, power, and control he wants, it's sittin' right here in Texas. There's so much of that glorious oil right off the shore. That's what he wants, and you know it."

"What are you proposing?" Aaron asked. His voice trembled.

"You strike them before they strike you. Mark my words, action against Texas is imminent," Callie said.

The word *imminent* seemed to echo and linger in the room as Aaron raked his hands through his hair and sighed loudly. "You want me to start a war? Have you lost your mind?"

"Have you lost your balls?"

Aaron laughed at the comment. "Still my righteous little sister, aren't you?"

"Think about it, Aaron. You know I'm right."

"Look," Aaron said. "I can assure you there isn't support for a war right now. Russo won't order troops into battle. You are acting emotionally. Why don't we both take some time to mourn the loss of Heather and Henry? What do you say?"

Callie rose from her seat. She went to the window and fidgeted with the curtain. The storm clouds hung low in the sky. A bolt of lightning jumped from one angry cloud to another. She faced Aaron, who sat upright in his seat as if deciding whether to remain seated or to stand with her.

"I say you tell Russo my story," Callie said, her heavy heart felt submerged in a pool of sorrow. "You tell him how I saw Everett's troops fire bullets into the backs of fleeing innocents. You tell him how I watched fucking bullets tear a fatal gash into Heather's head." Callie stopped. Her throat tightened and before she knew it, warm tears trailed down her face and dripped to the floor. "You tell him what I saw, Aaron. And then you tell Russo Texas will suffer the same fate." She turned away and wiped away the tears from her face.

Aaron hunched over, folded his hands below his knees with an expression she'd never seen before, one of pity. "Callie," he said. "I am so sorry this happened. I guess I shouldn't blame you. But what you are asking is impossible. Russo won't go for it. We should just—"

"Do you want to see the consequences of inaction?" Callie interrupted. "Just go to Eads. See for yourself."

Aaron blinked and said nothing.

She was losing him. "You represent Texas. And Texans fight," she said. "You've got to convince him."

"Is that what I say to President Russo, Callie? Texans fight? War is not brought about by clichés," Aaron said.

"But—" Callie started.

Aaron waved her off and pointed his bony finger at her. "No buts," he said. "You have nothing to offer. Russo will not give you bullets for sad stories. I've tried that already."

Outside, rain streaked down the expansive glass windowpanes as lightning cracked and unleashed a direct strike upon the earth. Thunder shook the room like an aftershock. Treetops wobbled violently in the strong wind as weak branches snapped under the pressure and fell to the ground.

Callie looked at her brother. He always made her feel like a child. He held some kind of power over her. Her mind scrambled—What had she to offer? Had she come to Texas to seek an end to the Reclamation Movement, or was it revenge that she tasted in the back of her throat? She thought of the moment in Eads where she played dead. While soldiers from the United States callously stood in fresh pools of Heather's blood, she auditioned for the role of a destitute coward. She remembered thinking if she had a weapon, she'd use it. Rage bubbled in her stomach. Any remaining pacifism she harbored unmoored from the dock of her soul. Justice for her sister was within her reach and she had to grab it.

She knew there was one thing more precious to the citizens of Colorado than even their lives—liberty. The exuberant passion for freedom from governance and dependence lived within her just as it had lived within those who chose to abide by the doctrine the flag of the Colorado Territory represented. It was the only thing any one of them proudly possessed, and it was the only thing she could possibly trade.

Callie faced Aaron. The tension of the moment canceled the emotion from her face. With a straight and even tone, she said, "I can offer our land."

Aaron tilted his head, in a gesture of intrigue. Of all the words that Callie could have said, it seemed these were the least likely.

"In exchange for your protection," Callie continued. "I am offering you an opportunity to form a government within the Colorado Territory that reflects the doctrine of the Texas Territory."

Aaron rose and paced the room, as he contemplated the offer. "Who gives you the authority?"

"Nobody gives anyone authority in Colorado," she replied. "However, our independence was recognized in a treaty with the United States. That treaty was broken when the US opened fire. Since there is no formal government within Colorado, the land is technically claimless. So, plant the flag of Texas before the United States plants theirs."

The pounding rain slowed to a drizzle and the trees stood erect again. Aaron looked out the window, staring across the Texas landscape.

"There is a border town between Kansas and Colorado that has very few people," Callie said. "I'd like to use your military to make a statement. Strike them first and let President Everett know the actions in Eads are a direct threat to Texas, and Texas will not go down quietly."

"A preemptive strike is war, Callie," Aaron said. "I just

don't—"

"Aaron, this will be a wakeup call to the US. We will be more effective at protecting our collective independence than waiting for it to be attacked."

"This is a provocative offer," Aaron mused. He walked to his desk, found a notepad and jotted down some words. Aaron smiled and glanced up from his pad. "Okay then," he said. A loose, pleasant tone returned to his voice.

"Do you think Russo will agree?" Callie asked.

"It'll take some convincing, but this is a very strong offer. If he accepts, we'll have ground troops ready in a day, and prepared to act on our command."

Callie took in her surroundings. She had spent four years living in a small community of pacifists with enough resources to get by. She imagined herself in Texas, protected by the well-armed citizens. An unfamiliar energy surged through her veins; the sensation was new, and she didn't recognize it. Then it struck her. The alluring sensation of power and prestige.

"Well, call him," Callie said, gesturing to Aaron's cell phone.

Aaron picked up his phone and dialed Russo.

10

Case and Renna walked toward the border. The golden grasses of the Colorado prairie folded and swayed with a gentle breeze as if the wind and the land had rehearsed this gilded dance. As the blades swayed, they scattered about a fresh, sunbaked aroma. The song of cicadas filled the air. Case could well have been five years old again, running through a field with his friend, Renna.

Just ahead, a river cut through the otherwise parched, brown land. The sun touched the canopy of green leaves above, casting irregular patterns of speckled light on the slow-moving water. Case knew this river well. It ran west to east, and if he followed it east, he'd end up in Kansas, now a border for the United States.

The river gave Case reason to pause, as the gravity of the situation settled on his shoulders. He was, after all, marching toward his imprisonment. Once in prison, he had no idea how he'd get out. He had spent his youth as an American citizen, and he was proud of that. But that was a different America, one that practiced tolerance. It was an America that would not have placed anyone in prison for opposing the government. His was an America in decline. Its decline was traceable to multiple generations spent growing government bigger and bigger under the pretense of safety, cradle-to-grave health care, the environment, and the military-industrial complex. Together, with the aid of giant corporations whose livelihoods depended on kickbacks, the elite government filled their coffers with money earned from unsuspecting citizens, only to spend it on things that suppressed freedom, choice, and as Renna had so eloquently expressed—love.

Case realized he was already in prison, a prison not made of iron gates, but one of stolen identity and free will. He, therefore, supposed that it didn't matter if his imprisonment was physical, as long as he was able to have a voice. And with that voice, he'd convince others to break the invisible barriers that imprisoned their minds.

Renna was the person who was listening to his voice. She was the person who would carry the torch into the United States, should his flame be extinguished. But Case couldn't be sure where she stood. He didn't know if she was ready to trust him. As such, he didn't know if he could trust her. He would be naive to assume that a few hours alone together could change beliefs that had been ingrained since birth. All he knew was Renna possessed a spark of doubt; and a spark was all it took to ignite a fire. Renna most likely knew if Eads had been a target. If she were to tell him classified information, he would know she trusted him. That trust would be good enough to give him hope. It had to be enough. If Callie was dead, Renna was the only person left.

"Renna," he said. "You mentioned your intel had me in Eads."

Renna nodded. "Yes, that's right."

"What was the purpose of your mission?"

"Our mission was to stop the advancement of energy

production within the Colorado Territory. Everett believed it brought with it the ability to produce weapons," Renna answered.

"Before your brigade dropped bombs on the windmills, I was on my way to the border to diplomatically prevent an attack on Eads. Do you know if the United States went into Eads?" he asked.

Renna exhaled and scanned her surroundings as she considered the question. "I've probably already said too much," she responded. "What you're asking me to tell you would be considered treason."

Case knew loyalty, when embedded from birth, was an extension of one's mind no different from using lungs to breathe. Renna was a victim of psychological manipulation, and he needed to explain the truth before they got to the border. If his negotiations failed and imprisonment turned into a death sentence, he'd have only her to be the new advocate for the Colorado Territory. If she didn't believe in him, she'd blend back into the fabric of military life. Case needed her to fray if there was a fiber of faith left.

Renna had strong doubt, he thought, but the instinct to conform under the pressure of a nation whose ground was fertile with the metallic gray of gun powder was not something many could handle. If she succumbed to the pressure, the idea of liberty would refract as easy as the light on the approaching river.

Case stopped at the river's shore. The river was at least thirty feet wide and the sound of rushing water filled Case's ears with a loud and constant *shusss*. A dichotomy raced through his mind. The sound of the river offered both a warning to turn around as well as a path forward. Though it would be easier to heed the warning he wouldn't. Freedom moves forward with adversity as its fuel.

The river's current careened with carelessness, and there was a lesson to be heeded in its flow. Despite copious amounts of bends and twists, the river always carried its water with incredible strength. Case was a leader, yet at times he believed his strength was as liquid as water. The muscles in his shoulders tightened again and he realized there was a slump to his form. He straightened his back, took a deep breath, and stretched his arms. His mind filled with fresh determination. This journey had stretched the muscles of his mental resolve to their limits, and mental satiation was as important as food.

Renna's gaze was concentrated on the river, presumably observing the current in her own way. She was stunningly beautiful, but, as with Callie, he buried his boyish excitement. Instead, he focused on the opportunity to teach Renna about the Colorado Territory.

"You know," he said. "Colorado has been my home my entire life. I know no other land."

Renna's lips were straight and her eyes shone brightly. Hers was a look of intensity and willingness to listen. "I know your story," she said.

"Do you?" Case asked.

"It's told to us," she answered.

"Tell me what they teach you."

"We're told how you stole our land," she said rather matter-of-factly. "By virtue of treaty, we were no longer permitted to continue oil and shale operations within the Territory. Since Texas owned production in the Gulf, we imported oil from foreign lands. The price of gas went so high that it shut down basic transportation operations. We also lost significant areas of western farmlands. The price of food went up as well. Coupled with the gas prices, the United States went into a deep depression."

"Is this my fault?" Case asked.

"They say you're greedy. They say you are holding back for payment," she said. "It was Everett who revitalized national interest by putting every last dollar into the Reclamation Movement. By contrast, you wanted us to starve and die. That is what was best for you, isn't it?"

Case shook his head. "No. That's not true. Is this why you enlisted?"

"It's the only job I could get," Renna replied. "If you join the military, you're taken care of. Three squares a day."

The heat of a late afternoon intensified, and Case's temple pounded with each beat of his heart. The wind whipped warm air across his face. The shade of a tree and the cool river presented an ideal resting spot. The border lay only a few miles from here and Case needed to ensure Renna was the person he needed her to be.

"Let's stay here for a bit," he said. "We'll be at the border in only a few miles and we're gonna need our energy." He sat under a tree and motioned for Renna to join him.

"Our perspectives are so different," Case said thoughtfully.

"What shaped yours?" she asked, sitting down next to him.

"Well, for the first two decades of my life, I knew a United States teetering on the edge of counterproductive civil discourse. You see, on its face, the differences within the two-party system were nuanced; each side jockeying for intellectual superiority over the other."

Renna listened closely.

"The purpose of these arguments was not of honest philosophical debate," Case continued. "It was for centralized control of the majority opinion. For whoever owned it, had the power."

"We're told our democracy is a representation of its people," Renna chimed in. "It's not a majority rule."

"It's supposed to be," Case answered. "But over time I developed a cynical view of our representative democracy. You see, representation of all people frayed into representation of fifty-one percent."

"So, time is spent pandering to one percent of the population who may harvest unpopular views?" Renna asked.

"Essentially," Case said. "And it lends credence to the

extremists found within both major political parties. Suddenly small pockets of violent radicals wielded a hell of a lot of power and influence. This fractional variance tore at the very core values of the nation. And when debate could no longer serve its purpose, persuasion was achieved in one of two ways: guilt by association, or when the Amarillo massacre happened, by the use of force and the subsequent fear, brought about by civil disobedience."

"Was that the moment?" Renna asked. "Amarillo? The start of the Second Civil War?"

Case nodded as he thought of that night. "When the People's Army of Texas struck back and the Battle of Amarillo broke out, my cynical view of democracy was confirmed. No longer would the government represent its people. It would serve only to fatten itself by consuming human spirits, no matter what side of the aisle you played for."

Renna closed her eyes and shook her head. It seemed Case planted an image in her mind that made her cringe. "So, what are you?"

Case laughed. It was such an interesting and appropriate question. "I'm an anarchist."

Renna chuckled at the statement. "You couldn't even kill me," she said. "Anarchy is a violent revolution."

"That's what those who wish to impose law, knowledge, and morals have led you to believe," Case said. "Any use of fear suggests control by an authoritarian figure or symbolic figurehead. Though some may masquerade as anarchists, they are in fact statists seeking to empower collective ideals, not yours. You see, violence and anarchy cannot coexist."

"I've not heard anything like that before," she said. Her tone filled the air with excitement, and her smile suggested an understanding.

"Of course you haven't. I never had, either. I just started thinking about governance from a philosophical perspective more than a practical perspective and that's when it started to make sense. That's when I knew I had to be the change, and I was the messenger."

"But your community," Renna said. "There isn't anything there; it's like you live on a commune."

Case laughed. "That's the last thing I ever wanted," he said. "It may seem that way, but in reality, all we did was live in freedom. Nothing was ever asked of our citizens. Nothing was ever forced. There was no governing document. As I had suspected, we gravitated toward the fulfillment of natural human needs. Obviously, we have to eat and sleep, but perhaps more importantly, we seek emotional connections with one another."

"What about those who don't do anything?" Renna asked.

"What about them?" Case responded.

"Why would you provide for them?"

"We don't do anything necessarily for each other," Case answered. "We did the things we could. As such there was plenty for everyone. Eventually, even those who could not plow fields sought connections with people and served an important role. Everyone's a philosopher in their own right, and a field of ideas is just as important as a field of food."

"So, who took care of the weakest among you?"

"No one, *per se*." Case replied. "We just took care of each other, without a second thought. For example, I am not a farmer, nor a rancher, but I never went without."

"This seems difficult to understand," Renna said. "You have no electricity or modern conveniences. Don't you miss these things?"

"Yes, I most certainly do," Case nodded. "But we have patience and many of us know a lot about technology. It's not like we had to invent fire again. With our combined knowledge, anything is possible. You know it to be true, because electricity was coming, right here in this very spot. Before the attack, that is. Once that happened, there would have been a vigorous return to all the things we once had. I believe within ten to twenty years we will have just as vibrant of an economy like any other."

Case looked around and noticed power lines in the distance. He pointed to them. "But it would have been different," he said with a smile. "It would have happened because of the human desire to achieve. You have to understand—emotional achievement is one of our natural instincts; money is inorganic. We were not born with the instinct to make money."

"But it is necessary," Renna insisted. "How can a society do without?"

"Don't misunderstand, Renna. Capitalism was the engine that brought humans out from the cold and into enlightenment. As ironic as this may sound, I believe that money eventually served only to slow progress."

"Really?" Renna asked with a tone of sarcasm in her voice.

"Well, as wealth is created, the desire to concentrate it within the government and among the wealthy precluded many from even entering the market of ideas. Startups were gobbled up, the competition was controlled or stifled, and money, or the need to protect it, acted as a noose to be tightened around your neck and not as a green field of plenty. You see this in the United States, don't you?"

Renna nodded. "I do. We all feel it, but what are we supposed to do about it?"

"Well, I'm doing something," Case said. "At least I'm trying. During the Second Civil War, I saw an opportunity to start this whole damn thing over. Only this time, I realized a system based on money would eventually cannibalize itself. We killed the cannibal and removed the noose around the necks of its believers. In fact, I called the people living within the Colorado Territory believers, not citizens. It was pure freedom, based truly on our natural, God-given rights."

Renna sat back and folded her hands in her lap. Her face turned stoic and her lips pursed. "Do you believe in God?"

"I do," Case replied.

Renna looked at him, the confused look on her face suggesting she needed more than a two-word answer. "Anarchists don't believe in God," she said. "They are skeptics at heart."

"I am a skeptic," Case said. "But I found that wherever I searched, and whenever I doubted, the path always wound toward God."

A Western Tanager landed on the banks of the river near Case and Renna. Its bright yellow chest caught Case's attention. The bird looked like a sunrise. It dipped its flaming orange head into the river for a refreshing bath before returning to flight.

"Come on, Case. What God could be so violent? Look behind you. Where is God among the rubble and bodies?" Renna asked.

"Not here. His is a path forward," Case said with a sigh. "Violence is not caused by God. Violence is caused by the desire to concentrate wealth and power. Without the influence of money, we are left alone to see God's gifts to us."

"People have been saying this for generations, you know," Renna said. "Yet, here we are again." The tone in her voice sounded small as if trapped, muted, and filled with doubt.

Above, the clouds found the sun and blocked its light. Goosebumps tickled Case's skin as the air seemed to instantly cool a few degrees. "I know," Case said. "It's why I cannot stop now. The Colorado Territory is the closest we've ever come to proving God's existence once and for all."

"How is that?" Renna asked. "How on Earth are you proving the existence of God?"

"Tell me, Renna, what is God?" Case asked.

Renna shook her head and glanced around. She looked up, no doubt noticing the sun blocked behind the cloud. "I guess God is a being, or perhaps an entity; all-knowing and all-powerful. The kind of thing you seem to be fighting against," she said.

Case laughed. "I didn't ask who *is* God. I asked *what* is God."

"I don't know," Renna said. "Who could know that answer?"

"It seems so easy to forget," Case answered.

"Well then," Renna said, her blue eyes shining with brilliance. "What is God?"

Do you remember the thing you said you can't find anymore in the United States?" Case asked.

Renna searched for words. Case sensed he was getting through to her, that she wanted to become a believer. "Love," she finally answered.

Case nodded. "We've all at one point said to ourselves that love is more important than money, especially in those times of need and despair. Yet, we cannot seem to give money up. Most of us believe that without money there would be no love. We would starve, we would be homeless, and we'd die young. I don't want you to believe in God if you choose not to, Renna, but I do want you to believe in love. You told me you believed in money, but do you believe in love?"

Renna's face was blank. There was a long pause. She tucked her head into her hands and gently sobbed. She glanced toward the river and wiped tears from her eyes. "No," she said. "I don't."

Case reached out and rubbed her shoulders. "Look at me," he said. Renna was reluctant at first but finally glanced at him. She was beautiful. "You can believe again. Love is the most abundant resource we have. In Colorado, we chose not to place value on currency, as it only would lead to hoarding, jealousy, and eventually hatred. We believe that passion can indeed drive innovation. Perhaps innovation happens a bit slower, but because of our raw human instinct to achieve, the end product is always of higher quality."

Renna nodded.

"The best part is, without currency no government can exist. It can't tax what is inside of you. It can't take away human instincts. Why would we even want to build something only to give it to the government? Every manufactured society— communism, socialism, capitalism, oligarchy, you name it, has proven time and again that they own everything. They all eventually take everything away from you. Why do this again, and again, and again? Why let them have it at all? The believers managed to efficiently provide for the community's needs with passion and love as the driving motivation. Maybe, just maybe, that's what God intended. That's what God means to me."

The white caps of the water in motion reflected within Renna's eyes. "What are you thinking?" Case asked.

"I'm just trying to absorb all this," Renna said. "It's a lot."

"Well, let me try to simplify it for you. As you watch the current, think about this—the motion of a river only stops when its source dries out," Case said. "The same can be said of ideas."

Renna sat quietly for a minute. She removed her shoes, rolled her pant legs up to her knees and let the water run over her feet. She seemed relaxed and contemplative. The wind carried away clouds and relinquished their gray grip on the sun's light. Bright rays once more reflected off the surface of the river and playfully bounced about.

For a moment, Renna was silent in thought. "There's a famous picture of you," she said. "I must've seen it a thousand times. It's of you signing the treaty with the United States. There's this look on your face—" she paused a moment. The river filled the pause with white noise. "It was the same look I saw in you the moment you decided to cast aside the stone you were going to kill me with."

"What look is that?" Case asked.

"The look on your face was very intense.," she said. "Your eyes were fixed on the treaty. Your stare was both intense and distant at the same time. I could just tell that you were contemplating the moment. I could almost see through to your soul. It was a look that suggested something bigger than the moment. Something important for the world; as if the pen used to sign the treaty was filled with your blood."

"It may well have been filled with my blood," Case answered with a laugh. The notion crossed his mind that perhaps signing the treaty itself was a mistake. It granted the Colorado Territory land, which was something of value and thus something to spar over. The realization left a pang within his stomach, that feeling of dread.

Renna gently splashed water over her exposed shins and took a deep breath. "What are you going to do when they put you in prison?"

"I'll request to speak with Everett," he said.

"And if he comes," she continued, "what are you going to say?"

"It depends a lot on his mood," Case said. "I guess I will be in the moment. All I know is I need to show the world the images of his doings here. People need to see the bodies and the gore. People need to see the reality of his destructive behavior."

"How are you going to do that?"

"I don't know yet," he answered. "A lot depends on you." Case removed his shoes and stepped gently into the river, allowing the water to race over his tired feet. The water was freezing, and his lungs tightened in response. The rapid water rushed against his aching legs. He waded up to his chest. The strength of the river pushed hard against his sturdy frame, blissfully cooling his inner core. He struggled to maintain his balance as drops of cold water splashed across his face. He opened his palms and let the water cleanse his wounds.

"Will you join me?" he asked.

"In the river?"

Case nodded. "It's very refreshing. It feels good on the wounds we've got on our palms."

She looked at him, intrigued. Her gaze trapped him like an animal, and Case could almost not comprehend her beauty. Suppressed feelings of passion pounded within, seeking urgent release. He couldn't let physical emotion overcome him, though. He fought his feelings with the fortitude of a tiger and the loneliness of a wolf, much like he had with Callie. His need for her acceptance was as powerful as his passion for the Colorado Territory. As the water healed him, he realized his destiny. He was going to die, and only in his death would the movement become recognized.

Renna's presence was far more serendipitous than anything

he ever experienced. She was not someone whom he coincidently rescued. He could feel it in his heart; she was the one to advance the message to the next generation.

Renna rose and unbuttoned her uniform. "I'm wearing spandex underneath. It's like a bathing suit," she said with a coy smile. "I could use the bath," she finished, as she stripped down to a layer of black spandex and entered the water. The sun lit her body as she tiptoed into the river, picking her feet up rapidly in the cold water. She ventured further in, breathing heavier with each step.

"Oh man," she said. "It's so fucking cold." She exhaled, smiled, and then splashed in the water like a teenager.

Case laughed, as he splashed the water gently about. "I know," he said through his chattering teeth. "I can't take anymore."

They exited the river and stood on the bank next to their clothes to dry off. Light found Case's skin through the treetops and it warmed him like a blanket. Renna opened her arms to the sun and spun around.

Case sat on the sandy bank. Renna moved close to him, so close that he could feel her skin brush up against his. Case drew a picture into the sand with a stick. It was the image on the flag of the Colorado Territory.

"Renna," Case said. "What does this image mean to you now that you see it again?"

Renna's eyes rapidly scanned the image. Case needed her to see the image as he did. The image represented liberty as a borderless presence of mind. It was tolerance of all thought, regardless of the acceptance of these ideas. It was the coalescing around these ideas and not a person.

Case needed her to understand what or who stood in their way. The enemy of liberty was the didactic speech of even a single individual in an attempt to amalgamate thought. The messenger of such language was always tempted toward authority and celebrity. Renna needed to reject such temptations, even if they came from Case's own mouth.

If she understood this, she would understand the image and subsequently, the peace and beauty of it all. If she didn't, the Colorado Territory would meet its demise. Renna rose and slid on her uniform. As she buttoned it, she offered Case a diffident smile. "I'm not sure that I can give you the answer you want," she said.

Case exhaled as the river water came in and partially washed the carved image away. "You told me that intel had me in Eads. Was Eads attacked?" Case asked for a second time.

She slid her boots over her dry socks, stood erect, and faced the border. "I'm scared to tell you, Case," she said bluntly.

"Scared of what?" Case asked.

"The consequences," Renna answered. "I know we are going to the border, and if they somehow learn I've leaked classified information, they would put me in prison as well. I don't want that. You should see how prisoners are treated."

"I won't say anything," Case said. For his plan to work, she should have trusted him enough to feel comfortable telling him this information.

"I don't know," she said. "Maybe you don't have to go. Maybe we could just stay here."

Case rose and stood next to her; his heart thumping at the prospect of staying in Colorado with Renna forever. Every powerful beat pumped hope into his veins. Hope was all he had left. "We can't stay here. There will be nothing here if we don't go now. Everett will reclaim it," he said. The words lingered in the surrounding air. It pained him to hear such a sad tone, as he was born to be the strong voice for the Believers of the Colorado Territory.

"I need you, Renna," he said. "I won't survive."

Renna wrapped her arms around her shoulders and rubbed them with her hands. She stared at the ground, her lips pursed, her face paling. Case shuddered at the cold, disapproving look.

"Of course, you won't. There is no more love," she said. "I

will help you get to the border. You can be my prisoner, but I can't promise what happens next. I don't want to die in prison, and I don't want to be left alone here. I think it's best for me to return to the life I am familiar with."

Case hung his head. He didn't think he could do it without her, but he had to try. "I understand," Case said, as they marched forward together.

A couple of hours later they approached the eastern border. The moonlight of the early evening lit the river like a silver ribbon. The bends of the river seemed to straighten as it faded into the pink shadows of the western horizon. It was all they needed to navigate the damp surface underfoot. Each step on the moist grass left behind impressions of a desperate march toward saving an idea still in its infancy. If Everett had his way, he'd sever the umbilical cord of this child still in the womb.

Up ahead a border agent held binoculars to his eyes. The agent made what appeared to be a frantic call on his walkie-talkie. Within a few minutes, more agents arrived fumbling with their binoculars.

"Now," Case said to Renna.

"Put your hands behind your back," she said to Case.

He complied.

She placed handcuffs around his wrists and secured them tightly. "It has to be real," she said.

"I know," Case answered.

There was the unsnapping of a holster and the soft sound of her weapon sliding loose. "Walk," Renna commanded.

Her sharp voice sent fear up Case's spine. Goddamn it if this were a ruse. She poked the gun into his back. "I said fucking walk."

Case obeyed.

Ahead, several guards ran toward them, automatic weapons at the ready. Case's legs quivered and he nearly fell over. Nothing he'd experienced prepared him for this.

"Stop!" a guard yelled. "Now," he ordered.

Renna pressed the gun harder into Case's back. He didn't know if it was intentional or just in fear. "My name is Private Renna Jensen of the United States. Hold your fire."

The guard moved closer. His weapon remained steady. He glanced at Renna. "You're from the States?" he asked. He was young and Case could tell by his tone he was nervous.

"Yes. I am Private Renna Jensen," Renna said and announced her platoon, commander, and mission. "I've come with a prisoner of war you'd all be interested in talking with." Her voice barked and echoed through the land.

"Private Jensen," the young guard chirped. "State the prisoner's name."

"Case Tappan of the Colorado Territory," she responded willingly and without hesitation.

The guards looked at one another and then directly at Case. "How did he escape Eads?" One of them asked, perhaps inadvertently. Case's heart sank deep into his chest with the realization that Eads was a target because of him. Renna told of his capture, leaving out the part where he saved her life.

The young guard moved within an arm's reach of Case. The guard's clean face showed no hint of beard growth and his dark brown hair was cut razor short. The innocence of his appearance suggested a weak persona, but the sturdy way in which he held his posture indicated he was willing to do whatever was needed to scrub this perception. The man's uniform had the US flag sewn into the sleeve. The number of stars was reduced, but it was otherwise the same. The number 97 was sewn below the flag.

"State your name," 97 ordered.

Case hesitated. Renna wasted no time pushing the gun harder into his spine. He winced and stated, "Case Tappan."

"Where are you from?" 97 asked.

"Eads, Colorado," Case said.

The young man smiled and engaged Renna. "This is good work, Private Jensen."

"Thank you, sir," she responded.

A second, older guard moved forward and spun Case around. "We'll take it from here," he said to Renna. "Report to medical for evaluation. There could be a medal in this for your efforts, Private."

A smile spread across Renna's face. It disappeared when she caught Case's glance.

"Where are you taking him?" Renna asked. There was a tone of purity in her voice. She understood they were not required to tell her.

"We'll keep him in Prison Bay One until we receive orders on how to proceed," 97 answered, nodding in the direction of a dimly lit red-brick building.

"I think Everett will be interested in knowing this right away," Renna said.

"I think you're right, Private," 97 replied.

The second guard motioned to 97 and they escorted Case to the prison. Case glanced back at Renna. Her posture was solid and stoic. Her eyes revealed nothing, and the light from a half-moon over Kansas concealed any emotions on her face.

11

Callie and Aaron entered the Capitol Building alongside the shadows of two security guards. The illuminated glory of the Texas state flag stood in the center of the rotunda. The folds of the dormant cloth hung like a head bowed in prayer within the quiet chamber. Five guards standing as points on a star around it kept watch as if the protected recipe for bravery, purity, and loyalty were woven into the fabric itself. Callie stopped at the flag and lowered her head. A warm wave of respect and humbleness entered her very core. Texas welcomed her home.

The guards escorted Callie and Aaron toward a glistening bank of silver elevators, the doors of which were ajar like they were hungry mouths anxiously awaiting food. Inside, there were no buttons or designations of floors. A guard held his badge against a reader, automatically engaging the lift. The doors sealed shut with a soft breath.

As the elevator rose, Callie's skin became clammy and her heart palpitated. In the next few minutes, she would be trying to convince President Russo to conduct a preemptive strike against the US. She hoped to get reassurance from Aaron, but his gaze was trained on the floor and his hands were folded in front of him. He bit his lip nervously. She wondered what role he was playing—protective older brother, or secretary of defense acting on a credible threat. She supposed it didn't matter, as long as she got her way. They rode the elevator for what seemed to be a long minute.

The elevator jerked to a stop. Its doors split apart and opened onto a wide hallway. The walls were painted a metallic, gun-metal gray and the crown molding and floor panels were blood red. The carpeted floor was charcoal black, creating an industrial feel of military prowess. Callie may well have been walking inside the barrel of a shotgun.

At the end of the hall was a set of double doors. Guards opened the thick doors inward. As Callie and Aaron entered, it was clear the room was reserved for meetings of high priority. Black leather chairs were tucked neatly under a round mahogany table. Above, a crystal chandelier shed its brilliant, glimmering light across the room. The gray, barren walls offered no opportunity for distraction. It seemed the only way to communicate with the outside world was a solitary red phone at the end of the table.

President Russo of Texas sat behind the red phone. His towering height was evident even when seated. He rose as Callie walked into the room, and she stared into his intriguing amber eyes. His eyes flicked like gold flakes in a riverbed when the light reflected off them at the right angle. He focused on Callie and somehow directed her with his intense stare toward the chair at the opposite end of the table. She had never been in the presence of someone so powerful before. His facial structure was the definition of perfect symmetry. His smooth brown skin showcased his youthful exuberance, yet heavy black stubble painted his face with refined purpose. Russo was familiar like a celebrity was familiar, yet human, like an average person waiting in line for a hot, steamy cup of coffee.

Callie maintained eye contact long enough for her to convey her physical attraction, but not too long so as to appear awkward. He rose and walked toward her; his light blue suit perfectly accentuating the even motion of his long legs as if he were born in it. He extended his hand and flashed a perfect smile.

Callie inhaled deeply. The mere act of shaking his hand might bring her to orgasm. She extended her arm and her fingers disappeared into his casual, yet firm, grip. She returned his smile and found herself held rapt by his gaze. Callie knew perfectly well that he sensed her attraction toward him, and he enabled it by lingering in the handshake and allowing her to behold his good looks a moment longer.

Behind her, Aaron cleared his throat. Callie had forgotten that her brother was even in the room. "Mr. President, may I introduce you to Callie Stanton," he said.

Russo nodded. "Ms. Stanton," he said, his voice deep and confident. "I've heard a lot about you already."

"Have you?" Callie asked, turning to Aaron. His face offered no hint of guilt.

"Won't you have a seat?" Russo said as he slid a chair out for her.

Callie sat and tucked her legs comfortably under the table. Aaron found his seat at the table next to Callie and Russo casually walked around to the other side and sat directly across from them both.

"Thank you for seeing me so quickly," Callie said, her nerves catching up to her, causing her hands to tremble. She placed them in her lap and squeezed her hands together.

"Yes, of course," Russo said. "I have been briefed as to the nature of the meeting, but I'd like to hear from you directly."

Callie's heart raced. She wanted to go into detail about the things she saw—the blood, the gore, the fear, the stone faces of young, the brainwashed soldiers, and the unjustified actions of the United States on the Colorado Territory, but she wasn't going to convince Russo with that story. He was a man who had presided over a civil war. She remembered what Aaron said. Russo was not going to exchange bullets for sympathy, so stories of dried bloodstains weren't going to convince him of anything.

Russo waited for a response. He sat motionless, like the subject of a portrait. Aaron shifted nervously in his chair. Callie knew she'd have to appeal to Russo as a representative of Texas and would have to adapt to his war doctrine. But as she gathered herself to speak, Callie's resolve weakened. Her body quivered, and her vocal cords wouldn't work.

In her head she heard the words Heather spoke in her final breath, *I'll die for this cause. Don't you let it be in vain.* The sentence echoed within her mind. Sweat beaded on her forehead as a sudden realization set in. Heather did not say, "don't let *me* die in vain." She had said, "don't let *it* be in vain." It was a subtle but important distinction. The word *it* could only have referred to the cause. Heather's life meant less than the cause. It's what Case had always espoused. Insecurity rained down on her insides and she felt sick. Was she representing Heather's wishes, or was she reacting emotionally, as Aaron had suggested?

She glanced at Russo but thought of Case's warm and sensitive smile. She knew his love for her was rivaled only by the passion for his ideology. Through their years working together, he told her of his feelings for her, yet he never acted on them. She pondered what would have happened if he had given his passion to her instead of his dogma. Had he listened to her, they'd be here together signing a treaty. Her stomach turned sick with a dose of potent jealousy. Case's commitment to Colorado had become a mistress rather than a pledge to a creed. Had he chosen to be with her, Eads would not have been destroyed and her sister would be alive. Callie couldn't help but feel that the blood of Eads ran to Case's doorstep.

Russo's eyes glimmered in the light. His face was serious, and he radiated a sense of security. He was a man. Russo protected his passion with something concrete, something metallic, something that could pierce the flesh of soft opposition. Russo was the man she had wanted Case to be all along.

She turned to Aaron and his eyes urged Callie to say something quickly. She opened her mouth, but her speech could not catch up with her emotions.

"Mr. President," Aaron said, wasting no more time. "Allow me to discuss the nature of this meeting."

Russo waved him off. "Ms. Stanton," he said in a tone directing her to speak.

Callie scanned the gray walls of the room looking for anything to stop her mind from wandering. On the contrary, the barren room offered no such luxury. Callie's scrambled emotions and snarled mind coalesced at once. "Mr. President," she said. "The Reclamation has begun, and Texans are in danger."

Her first words spilled from her mouth and seemed to skate across the shiny mahogany table and land directly into Russo's open hands.

Russo made a fist as if closing her sentence into his large grip. There was no going back now. "Why should I believe Texas is in danger? We've already signed a treaty that ceased the civil war with the United States," Russo said.

"We had a treaty too," Callie answered. "It seems to me Everett is not one to obey treaties."

"But you had nothing to back up your treaty. No government, no weapons, nothing worth a damn other than an idea," Russo retorted. "He'd be a fool to disobey our treaty, don't you think?"

Callie was prepared for this argument. "I should remind you that Everett ran and won an election on reclamation. Do you honestly think he'll be satisfied with Eads? Do you think he'll stop at Telluride? Or do you think he's got his eyes on the Gulf?"

Russo folded his arms across his chest, leaned back in his chair, and looked away from her for the first time since she entered the room. "What do you recommend, Ms. Stanton?"

Callie paused for a moment, willing Russo to look back at her. She knew what to say, and she just needed to say it. "A preemptive strike."

It was done. Her body was like jelly and she could almost taste the residual sourness of her words. If Case had heard her utter "A preemptive strike," he surely would have gotten up and left the room. Nothing she'd ever said seemed as powerful as those three words. She inhaled and strength returned to her body. She sat upright and placed her steady hands on the table. Aaron nodded in agreement, and Callie could tell that he was proud she'd finally said it.

Russo tapped at the table and shifted in his seat. "And why should I do this?"

"To send a message to the United States that civil war will be the only way to take our land," Callie said with steady resolve.

Russo sat back with cautious ease and shook his head. "This is too risky," he argued. "I presided over the end of the last civil war, and you have not convinced me that I need to provoke another. Everett has not violated our treaty as of yet. They are taking your land, not ours."

"Actually," Callie said. "I'm prepared to negotiate land."

"Negotiate land?" Russo said with a laugh. "What could you possibly have to offer that hasn't bled out already?" Russo asked. "You can keep Eads."

"I am offering more than Eads," Callie said.

Russo's glance rose from the table and locked with hers. She melted into his gaze and her legs shook once again. "What then?" he asked, his voice booming in the room like thunder.

"I am offering you an opportunity to form a government within the Colorado Territory that reflects the doctrine of the Texas Territory. This includes not only Colorado, but New Mexico, Wyoming, Montana, Idaho, Nebraska, and the Dakotas. If we achieve this, I believe we will be more effective at protecting our collective independence from the United States," Callie said. Her legs stopped shaking and she took a moment to breathe normally. "Together, we will control more wealth, more land, and more resources. Everett will have no choice but surrender to us, or else face continued economic devastation."

Russo's face relaxed. "Who gives you the authority?"

Callie looked at Aaron. Oddly, he lowered his head and shifted in his seat. He seemed agitated. "Who gave us the authority to sign a treaty with the United States? No one," Callie retorted. "Who gives anyone authority in a place with no government? No one. I guess the better question is who stops me?"

Without another word Russo sat back in his chair, arms folded across his chest. The only sound was breath.

"I've drafted an agreement," Aaron said, displaying the contract on the table. "It's all laid out."

Russo retrieved the contract and reviewed it. Callie watched his eyes rapidly scan the words. Words she knew would forever change history. The emotionless room could not contain the excitement that replaced her nerves as she stifled a smile.

Russo flipped through the document. When he had finished reading, he lifted his head and drew in a deep breath. "When would you need troops?" he asked.

"Immediately, sir," Callie replied.

Aaron produced three pens and handed one to each. "Is this a deal?"

Russo took his pen and casually flipped it through his fingers before resting it in his right hand. "It is clear to me, Ms. Stanton, that the massacre in Eads was an egregious and intolerable act of inhumanity. The actions of President Everett are that of a tyrant who speaks only for himself and not of the ideals of the people he purports to represent. As such, actions against United States military bases which pose a direct threat to the rights of those of us in Texas are warranted and justified." Russo spoke frankly and without emotion.

"I can assure you," Russo continued. "We will neutralize the threat the United States poses to the Colorado Territory, as it will become the property of Texas." With that, Russo signed the agreement.

Aaron signed next and then slid the treaty to his sister. Callie picked up the pen. It felt heavy and awkward in her hand.

She examined the unreadable signatures of Russo and Aaron drying on the thin paper. Her hands shook as she finished the final stroke of her signature. She placed the pen in her pocket as a memento. Her eyes met the smiling face of Russo. His look was warm and inviting. Her heart fluttered and she playfully ran her fingers through her hair as she tried to retain a straight face.

"The Kansas border has agents," Russo said. "I will order a small, targeted attack in response to the oppressive activities that occurred in Eads. Do you agree with this decision?"

"Yes sir," Aaron started. "I suggested this in the past and appreciate—"

Russo waved him off. "Ms. Stanton, do you agree with this decision?"

Callie nodded. "Yes sir," she answered.

Russo picked up the phone's red receiver and ordered the strike.

12

Case was escorted into Prison Bay One where the guttural moans of several caged prisoners echoed against dreary and ordinary red-brick walls. The sounds were dark and disturbing, like those of desperate animals in despair. Case cringed at the sounds and his heart felt like a large syringe had sucked the blood from its chambers.

A man rose and latched his fists around the iron containment bars. His eye sockets sat back in his skull, his gray hair was disheveled, his skin was wrinkled, and his features were darkened by dirt and sorrow. All that remained of his withering body was loose skin, which appeared ready to slough off his weakened bones in a heaping, goopy pile of blood and muscle. There was no salvageable life in his deep green eyes. The look on his gaunt face was not one that cried for help, but one of sad acceptance. It said to Case it was only a matter of time before a similar fate would be bestowed upon him.

As they walked through the blisteringly hot facility, 97 pushed a weapon into Case's back with such force that pain rocketed up his spine. He suspected this would be his new normal; a day without pain would be one to celebrate. They passed a rickety oak desk with papers strewn across it. A guard rose from a backless stool and followed them. The second guard wore a set of keys attached to his belt with a strong metallic cord. The number on his uniform read "26" and he handled the keys as if he were holding gold.

"Unlock this cell," 97 ordered 26.

The guard nervously fumbled for the one that unlocked the door. It took him a few times to find the keyhole. The lock popped with a sharp click and the heavy door opened with rusty resistance. A sharp scraping sound sliced through Case's already aching head. Guard 26 nodded and walked away. Guard 97 shoved Case in and slammed the iron door shut with a heavy thud. Case turned and looked at 97, his face partially obstructed by the iron bars.

"A meal will be here in a few hours. If you gotta piss, there's a hole over there," 97 said, pointing to the back corner of the tiny cell.

Case noticed an actual hole in the ground that led to God-knows-where. Steam emanated from its depths and its foul scent found its way to Case. He crinkled his nose in disgust. Case glanced at 97. A sinister smile lay across his face.

"You're one of them now," 97 said as he turned and disappeared into the darkness of Prison Bay One.

A yellow incandescent bulb dimly lit the windowless cell. Everything appeared shadowy and filthy. Case looked around and noticed a man sitting upright on the bed. The man rose and walked toward Case. The name "Walls" was sewn into what remained of his shabby, white-and-black uniform.

Walls stared at Case. He smelled of body odor and decay. Case expelled a violent cough as his lungs rejected the stale air of death.

"You are one of us now," he said, repeating 97's words with a foreboding tone of certainty in his deep, dark voice.

"I guess I am," Case said. Acceptance settled in like a weighted blanket on his chest.

The groans of other prisoners settled down. Perhaps the sheer sight of a guard brought with it the possibility of eating, and the moans were ferocious hunger pangs.

Walls stood next to Case, gripped the iron bars, and looked into the empty hallway. He puckered his cracked lips and whistled an unfamiliar song. The notes were flat and out of tune. The shrill sound shot through Case's ears. Case tapped rigorously on the cold iron cage with his pointer finger—he wanted out.

Mercifully, the whistling stopped. "What are you in for?" Walls asked, keeping his distance.

It didn't matter what Walls knew. "I'm a prisoner of war," Case said.

"What war?" Walls asked.

Walls would have no idea of any news from the outside world. "The United States has attacked the Colorado Territory."

Walls inhaled deeply and spoke slowly. "I guess I saw that coming," he said. "I'm here for defection."

"Defection?" Case asked. "Meaning trading secrets?"

"No," Walls said. "I tried to cross into Colorado."

After the Amarillo War, the nature of defection had changed in these United States of America. The simple thought of resistance was akin to defection. It was a brutal and unjustified use of government force and manipulation of thought.

"Did you stand trial?" Case asked.

Wall's lips stretched into a thin, sarcastic smirk. "Defection is punishable without due process. We are a threat to national security."

"We?" Case asked.

Walls cast his emaciated arm out of the cell and pointed at the other captives. "This entire place is occupied with the souls of the innocent trying to cross the border and make a new life in the Colorado Territory."

"Rise up boys," Walls called, "Show yourself." His voice reverberated against the brick building.

The prisoners rose and clambered into the faint light. Shadows from the bars slipped across their bodies. From what Case could see, they were all at various levels of decay. Case's heart pounded rapidly. "Jesus," was all he managed to squeak out.

Walls turned back toward Case. Walls' pupils opened wide, absorbing any light they could. "It won't take long before your body deteriorates. The food is meager and comes at different times each day, if at all. You'll lose thirty pounds in the first month. Your energy will disappear, followed by your will. Even if we were to try to run, our bones would shatter, and we'd collapse."

"This is torture," Case said. His legs felt weak and his hands tremored. Was this his fate? Was this how it ends?

"Yes," Walls replied. "But that's not the most disturbing thing about this place."

Case shuddered. "Physical torture?"

Walls shook his head. "No. With so much suffering in this prison, you think you'd see the good in people. You'd think even one guard would sneak us something to eat. No. What the United States does to us is neglect. What they do to the minds of their citizens is torture."

Suddenly, bright sunlight filled the prison from its entrance. Case shielded his eyes from its incredible glow. 97 entered the prison, ran to the desk, and frantically shuffled paper into its drawers. He looked up and glanced around the room. His eyes widened as he noticed all the men at their gates. He placed his hand on his holster and walked to the middle of the room.

"What's goin' on?" he barked.

There was no response.

"Why are you all standing?" 97 said, walking closer to Case. "Is it to see the new guy? You all so damn curious? Do you think he's special? Do you think he's strong? You think he's gonna get you out?"

The guard looked directly at Case. His eyes were deep blue, and they only served to enhance his youthful appearance. "This is your hero," he said directly to Case, as a bit of spittle frothed at the corner of his mouth.

Sunlight kissed the room for a second time as two figures entered the room. When the door shut, Case saw Renna and guard 26. She had donned a clean, new uniform of the United States Army. She studied the room, glanced at Case and quickly looked away. At that moment, Case knew he'd lost her.

Guard 97 didn't turn to acknowledge the presence of Renna and 26. His laser blue eyes never broke from Case's. "This is Case Tappan. He's the leader you were all trying to escape to. Ain't that funny? There ain't anywhere for you to go now. Even if the idea was festering within those rancid brains in your saggin' skulls, just know that your leader is as good as dead. It won't be long before he looks like you. It won't be long before he acts like you, and it won't be long before he thinks like you. 'Cause this is what you deserve—to die here next to the man who stole our land and made it impossible to do so much as feed you. You blame him now. Not me. I'm certain if any of you had the strength, you'd beat the shit out of him. I'd like to, but what fun would that be? More fun to just watch him dissolve away, like all the rest of you."

Guard 97 mercifully broke eye contact with Case, turned and noticed Renna in the room. "Private," he said, acknowledging her with a salute. Renna saluted in return.

The guard slowly walked toward Renna, making certain to look at each of the prisoners as he spoke. "Private Jensen here is to thank for Mr. Tappan's capture. You see, she was out serving this fine country of ours, not defecting from it. In fact, she's gonna get a hero's welcome from a very special someone. You see, Mr. Tappan here has an admirer." He stopped for a moment, laughed, and shook his head. "Well, I can't call him a fan. A better term would be an adversary of the highest-ranking.

President Everett. And he's here now."

A buzzer sounded and the yellow light in the room flickered. As the light blinked, skinny silhouettes of human figures behind bars appeared against the walls. The entrance flung open with force, and a beam of light from the outside world flooded the dank prison. The shadowy outline of President Everett stood blocking the glory of the day's brightness. He paused for a moment, allowing people to soak in his presence, and then moved away from the light. The door sealed shut with a sturdy clunk.

Everett walked slowly down the aisle and surveyed his prison. He wore a black army uniform adorned with the highest degree of gold and silver symbols representing his role as Commander in Chief. His salt-and-pepper hair, cut to the top of his ears, was perfectly arranged. He sold the appearance of certainty, even if uncertainty fed the mood. His stout legs and upper body were muscular and filled out his uniform completely. His face showed the wisdom that comes with age but bore the wrinkles of stress brought about by the rigors of leading a flailing nation. Despite this, his casual strides exuded confidence. Perhaps the failures of the Reclamation Movement were by design so destitute Americans were forced to seek the power of its leader for a glimmer of hope.

Everett made sharp eye contact with Case. His boots clicked on the hard floor as he came closer to him. His lips curled into a smile and he drew a deep breath. "Mr. Tappan," he said. "It is a pleasure to finally meet you."

Case's stomach soured and his body shook. The tone in Everett's dark voice was condescending, sinister, and filled with disdain. Case did not extend a welcome in return.

"Nothing to say?" Everett said. "I am so disappointed. I was hopeful for at least a smile, or perhaps a lecture. Maybe you'd like to tell me all about the great Colorado Territory. Maybe you'd like to tell me about how beautiful the lives are of the very people that raped and stole my land."

Case cringed. Everett's gaze held him in some kind of trance. His body was trapped behind bars, and his desire to save the Colorado Territory was trapped within Everett's evil and unrelenting mind.

"There's a treaty," Case said calmly. "You violated it, not us."

Everett looked Case up and down. "The treaty was never authorized by the United States Senate, and even if it were, my friend, I couldn't give a shit about it. A contract between nations is nothing when it cannot be enforced with bullets."

"That is where you've got it wrong," Case said. He straightened his back and did not look away from Everett's powerful glare. "The spark of liberty isn't threatened by bullets. It can't be killed. You see—when it feels as though all is lost, liberty will be that which thrives."

"From which one person will eventually rise to power by the simple offer of aid," Everett said. "She'll pool the wealth and decide how it is dispensed. Of course, she'll have to protect that wealth with something, don't you think? It is simply human nature, Case. People look for leaders, and leaders feed on power."

"We were the first to prove that wrong," Case shot back. "We were the first to perform outside the vacuum of old money. We were the first to demonstrate that evolution of the instinctual need to seek protection from the storm under someone else's umbrella has changed. We toiled in whatever capacity we could and offered it to each other and we served one another. We proved leadership is contained within, and no one person has the right to take control of it."

"Oh, I agree no one has the right to take control of it," Everett said, his smile widening. "You see, I don't have to take control. People give it to me willingly because it's easier to place their burdens on my shoulders than to carry it themselves. And I know how to deliver. You know this to be true, Case. You are a leader, aren't you? You can feel that power growing inside of you right now. You are persuasive and convincing. You are no different than me. Isn't that true, Mr. Tappan?"

Case knew how that feeling of power was like a drug, addicting at its first taste. True resistance is found deep within. Liberty is the antidote of power, and once the source is discovered, it feels even better than the most powerful drug, and Case was hooked.

"You can't stand it," Case said, gripping the bars so tight his hands ached. "This is why you wanted to see me, isn't it? You can't stand to be wrong. While your livelihood depends on the submission of a misinformed populace gravitating toward self-destruction, we proved that people do not self-destruct without external circumstances giving them any other option. We showed you something far more devastating than bullets to a dictator like yourself. We showed you that people inherently gravitate toward well-being. Not perfection, mind you, but virtuousness.

"Perhaps more frightening to you is that we accept this notion and portray it as a moral obligation. As it turns out, the self-destruction you speak of is manufactured by people whose only reality has been molded from birth about the supposed benefits of government. As such, government royalty must perpetuate this disillusion through whatever soul-sucking means possible, and to admit otherwise would be the end of its power. You see, Mr. President, I don't need governance, and I don't need a leader. This is why you feel threatened, isn't it?"

Everett placed his hands on the bars above Case's and leaned in; his face nearly touching the iron. "I guess you're right," Everett said with a sneer. "Your family in Eads certainly doesn't need a leader anymore."

Anger surged through Case's veins. His heart pounded rapidly. "You can kill liberty's people, but the history is written. It only takes a small torch to revive it. I am asking that you let it live in harmony with you."

Everett laughed. "Live in harmony? Is this a joke?"

"It's not a joke. I can show you," Case said. "First, stop the attacks."

"My friend, it is not I that you first need to convince," Everett said.

"What do you mean?" Case asked.

"We've detected troop movement headed to the border."

"What troop movement?"

In the dim yellow light, Case caught a glimpse of 97's smug face. His little eyes filled with antagonism and he nodded at Case. Case looked at Renna's emotionless face. She was listening, but there was no reaction, just like a good soldier.

Everett backed away from Case's cell and took two steps toward the exit. "The troops are from Texas. They have entered the Colorado Territory and appear to be headed in this direction. Are they coming to rescue you?"

Confusion ripped through his brain. "No," was all he could manage.

"There is no other reason, Mr. Tappan. Of course, this all smells of war to me. Might you have something to do with this? If they are not coming for you, then perhaps you've arranged for this."

"I wouldn't," Case answered. He searched his mind for any rational reason this would be happening. He noticed a reaction from Renna. Her jaw hung open for a moment and then she quickly regained a proper posture.

"You do know who the secretary of defense for Texas is, right?" Everett said. "Aaron Stanton. Is the name familiar?"

Case knew it was Callie's brother. He closed his eyes. Could it be she had something to do with this? Could it be that she was there, among the troops? He wished he could warn her that Everett knew. She was in danger.

"I know what you are thinking," Everett said. "Everyone died in Eads." His voice was quiet and husky. "Unfortunately, we don't know what became of Callie Stanton. We were unable to identify her among the bodies."

Case inhaled deeply, seeking calm from the oxygen. The prisoners stirred and someone struck a hanging incandescent bulb causing the light to sway back and forth. Shadows dipped about the prison as if they were all trapped on a stalled fishing vessel bobbing helplessly in the ocean's waves.

"Calm down," guard 97 called out as his gaze danced from cell to cell; his hand gripping his holster, ready to maintain order.

Everett remained unfazed. "Troop movement is an act of war and is exactly what the citizens of the United States need to see. Unity with Texas will confirm to the citizens of the US that Colorado is more than a docile territory. On my command, our armed forces will eliminate this threat and this prison. I have informed the media as well. I suspect there will be full coverage. The American people need to see just how savage this collusion between Colorado and Texas has become. We will have it all back now."

Without waiting for a response, Everett walked away from Case. "Guards," he called. His voice echoed throughout the prison. "You will have one hour to vacate. After that, your safety cannot be guaranteed."

Everett prepared to exit the prison and stopped when he noticed Renna raise her hand in salute. "You must be Private Jensen."

"Yes, Mr. President, sir," she answered. Her stance was stiff and stoic.

"I am to understand you are the one who brought Case here."

"Yes sir," she answered like a well-trained dog.

He reached out and placed his hand on her shoulder. "At ease," he said. Renna lowered her hand, and her body relaxed.

"I've ordered a special convoy to retrieve you in half an hour. They will take you to Washington, where you will be one of the recipients of an achievement star and a guest of mine at the reception to follow."

"Yes, sir. It will be an honor."

"If we're lucky, by the time dinner is over, The United States will have reclaimed the Colorado Territory completely. What a historic day, don't you think?"

"Yes sir," she said with a smile. Her gaze skimmed Case's. "It certainly is."

"Very good," Everett said, removing his hand from Renna's shoulder. "Be safe, Private."

Light flooded the prison once again, as Everett's shadow filled the rectangular outline of the open doorway. The door slammed shut and the room was met with silence.

Guard 97 broke the silence with a sharp clap of his hands. "Men," he said to the guards. "I see no reason to linger. Grab your gear and get the fuck out of here." He noticed Renna. "Congratulations, Private. Your convoy is already waiting for you in Hangar One. You'll be in DC in under three hours. Move out." Guard 26 exited the building and 97 returned to the desk and removed files from its drawers.

Renna turned, looked at Case, and walked out the door. Case closed his eyes. His shoulders slumped and his hands slipped down the iron bars with a loose grip. There was a brief moment in which the air stood still and no one moved. In that moment, Case was suspended in time. His presence was distant and contemplative as if he could view his own visage. He saw the face of a man who knew these were the last moments of his life. His brain spun the irony of spending his last hours behind bars after a lifetime devoted to freedom. Yet, throughout history, brave pioneers spent their final moments as prisoners. Only in death could the possibility of a second coming exist; one which peaceful people walk among each other again.

Silenced, Case walked toward his cot. He heard the scuffle of feet and the sound of cot springs as other captives retreated as well, some perhaps soothed by the idea that their torture will soon come to an end. Theirs was a conclusion whose moral of the story preached the false virtue of acceptance as the ultimate sacrifice.

Case sunk into his cot and stared at his bleak surroundings. The yellow lights of the prison creaked as they swung in a stale air circulated by a large overhead fan whose motor whirred with the occasional clunk of resistance. Above the desk, the white-faced clock with black Roman numerals and linear marks clicked as the minute hand moved forward. Case watched the minute hand advance again and again and again.

From the dimness emerged a light from the prison door. The guard glanced over his shoulder. "What are you doing here?" 97 said, his tone was high pitched and confused.

The shadow of an arm raised up and a weapon was visible in the light. "What the fuck are you doing?" 97 said. He rose and reached for his holstered weapon.

A gunshot rang through Prison Bay One. Case felt its retort curl through his eardrums and reverberate in his head. He raced to the front of his cell just in time to see 97 slump to the floor, the bloody remains of his head scattered on the desk. The shooter knelt by 97 and seemed to be rummaging around his uniform.

The shooter rose with the set of keys retracted from 97's belt and ran toward Case. His eyes opened wide and his body surged with intense energy as he realized it was Renna. She wore civilian clothes, a plain white T-shirt and black stretch pants. Case saw a black bra underneath her shirt. She arrived and fumbled with the keys. She was sweating and Case's heart accelerated as he watched her bright blue eyes shift with uncertainty. Behind those eyes, was a woman struggling with acceptance. Her conscience conflicted with the people she was supposed to trust.

"Renna," he said. "I thought you were gone."

"I got on that plane," she answered. "I was ready to go." She tried one of the keys and it didn't fit, she fanned the keys out in her hand like a deck of cards and selected the next one. "Then I started thinking about all the things you told me, and it hit me."

The key failed to open the lock. "What hit you?" Case asked.

"The question you asked me about," she replied.

"The question?"

"You know when we were still in Colorado? You asked me

what the image of the Colorado Territory meant to me."

"I remember."

She selected the third key. It didn't work. "I know how to answer it."

Renna tried the fourth key without success. "How many fucking keys are there?" She mumbled to herself. "We've got no more time."

The commotion aroused the prisoners and they walked to the front of their cells. Walls watched with particular intrigue. "Are you going to get me out?" he asked.

"I'm trying," Renna said. The next key failed to unlock the cell.

"Case," she said. "That image on your flag means nothing to me." She inserted the next key and the lock sprung open.

Case pushed the door open and stood next to Renna. Case looked at her, "You do understand," he said.

"It means absolutely fucking nothing," Renna said, as a smile crossed her face. "What I do know is that it feels right to help you, and I choose to do so under no duress from the image on your flag. I chose to do so by my own free will. Your flag means nothing to me."

Case moved forward, opened his arms and wrapped them around Renna.

Walls limped out of his cell. "I have no idea what you two are talking about," he said, "but, can we get the others out?"

"How much time do we have?" Case asked.

"Not much," Renna said. "I know the troops from Texas are in position, and Everett has authorized an airstrike. It could happen at any moment. The intel I overheard suggests that Texas troops are within walking distance from Prison Bay One. An airstrike will devastate their unit."

"We have to warn them," Case said, once again thinking of Callie.

"Wait. Can you let my friends out first?" Walls said.

Case looked at a prisoner across from him. The prisoner

raised his arms to his side with both palms opened. "You gonna free us?" The prisoner asked. "You gonna set us free into this world?"

The prisoner was thin-set and his skin looked like a plastic doll that had been tossed into a hot oven. "Yes. You are free now," Case said, as Renna opened his cell.

The alleged defector slowly moved forward and stopped. "I heard what is goin' on," he said. "There's no freedom as long as they have bombs." He stepped one foot into the hallway and looked at Case. "Just as much as there is no liberty as long as they have jails."

Case hesitated. "I just opened your cell, didn't I?"

"But there are still bombs," he said and exited the prison.

Renna finished opening all the cell doors. The men walked freely and found their way out.

"Am I gonna face God?" One of the men turned and asked Case.

"I don't know," Case answered.

"I'm a sinner," he said. "The cell kept me straight."

"Then you're best to turn your life around and start to live right," Case said, looking directly at Renna. "Or make it right."

"There is no making it right," Renna said. "You've got to live with your choices. Your burdens may never go away; they just become a part of who you are."

The newly freed prisoner nodded and walked out.

Walls lingered. A look of dejection soured his thin face. He retreated to his cell and pulled the gate shut. The lock clicked.

"What are you doing?" Case asked.

"Just leave me here," Wall's weak voice muttered. "All this time here. I'm scared of freedom. It's better this way."

"What? You can't," Case said, trying to pry his locked cell open again. "Renna, give me the keys."

Renna pulled at his arm. "Case," she said. "It's time."

"Give me the keys," Case pleaded.

She handed the keys to Case. Case threw them into the cell,

and they landed on the floor with a clink. "It's your choice now," Case said.

Walls looked at the keys and then at Case. "Show the world, Case Tappan," he said. "Show the world."

"We gotta get out of here," Renna said, pushing Case. "Now."

13

Case and Renna emerged from Prison Bay One. Clouds hid the sun and the dull and dreary day hung so thick in the air Case may well have been wearing the clouds on his skin. The upward trajectory of sturdy tree trunks wound wearily toward the sky as their tops stealthily disappeared into the clouds. On any other day, it would have been a mysterious, serene, and dreamy setting. Today, however, Case sensed an eerie yearning for a return to stability and sanity. As if nature wanted to capture the ills of corruption in its white grip and escort it out to sea. Case's head ached with uncertainty as he was struck by the opposing forces of majesty and desolation. He reached out and touched Renna's shoulder.

The surrounding grounds of the military base were silent and there was a stark absence of activity. All of the United States border agents had vacated.

"That's the way to Colorado," Case said and pointed west.

As Case and Renna walked westward, the fog settled into the totality of a white abyss. They tried to continue, but Case could see no farther than the backs of his own hands. He turned his hands over and observed the healing fortune lines etched into his palms. Within those lines lay the story of his triumphs, his failures, and his death; the latter of which he figured was moments away.

He reached for Renna's hand and held it in his. Her skin was warm and welcoming. When he touched her, there was a certain peace contained within her being that reached the very core of his soul. Something akin to an electric shock coursed through his veins as he came to the impulsive realization that peace was the foundation of human essence. All other experiences only served to alter that foundation either for good or for bad. This fundamental peace can only be tainted to the extent one's experiences allow. The Reclamation Movement was an experience in tyranny, and it was no different than the creeping malignant fingers of a brain tumor attacking and eating the peaceful resting state of the human mind from the inside out.

Renna's blue eyes appeared through the gray skies as they had from the blanket of ashes when they first met. If he could read the thoughts behind those eyes, they would likely be the same as his—What is the cure for a philosophical cancer that has ruled the earth since the dawn of time?

A brook babbled with an inconsistent flow. A flock of birds scattered in unison; their familiar chirps noticeably absent. The fog enveloped him like a ghost wrapping its cold arms around his body. The only thing that kept him grounded was the temperateness of Renna's hand and the belief that the future would reserve a spot for them both at the dinner table of history.

Case slowly crept forward with the sensation of the despotic eyes of President Everett upon him. He was the man standing in the middle of nations and his next actions could trigger destruction.

A drizzle escaped from saturated clouds. The drops were like tiny needles on his exposed skin and the woodsy smell of musty and damp trees permeated his nose. They were lost.

Renna remained hushed but held a look of resolute purpose and confidence. She was not lost at all. She looked ahead.

She motioned toward the sound of the river. She leaned in close, and Case felt the heat of her breath in his ear as she whispered, "If we follow it, it may lead us to them. We can stop this." Case nodded and they moved forward together. A sense of ease set about his body, and he walked with purpose. Renna was everything the Colorado Territory ever needed. Just like she physically held the key that sprung him from his prison cell, her curiosity and tenacity held the door open so the next mental prisoner of oppression could escape.

The wind stirred the hidden leaves in the trees and the drizzle coated his face with a thin layer of moisture. They followed the trail blazed by the river. In the near distance, Case heard the distinct clank of a soldier's gear. He froze in place and listened intently. The noise grew louder.

"It's them," he whispered to Renna. "It's Texas."

Case and Renna moved toward the soldier. Each step carefully selected so as not to be heard. The gray shadowy outline of an individual moved within the fog then suddenly stopped. Gently, the natural bend in his arm transformed into a ridged extension as he slowly lifted a rifle into position. Case knew the soldier could see them. He raised his arms in a motion of peace.

"On the ground," the soldier called. "Now."

Case threw his body onto the muddy surface and placed his hands behind his head. Renna fell next to him, her breath just as rapid as his. The soldier arrived within seconds and dug the barrel of his weapon into the small of Case's back.

"Please," Case said. "My name is Case Tappan. I need to speak to your sergeant. You are in danger."

"Stand up. Both of you," the soldier said. "And keep your fucking hands over your head or I will shoot you."

Case and Renna did as they were told. Case cocked his head around and caught a glimpse of the young soldier. The soldier's gaze jumped from tree to tree, and he bore the naiveté of one who believed he could die. Unlike the American soldiers whose faces wore the skin of the most sophisticated psychologically-prepared military ever devised, and the mask of one who accepted death as inevitable.

The guard looked Renna up and down. Her foresight to change out of her uniform was more than likely the only reason they were not dead. "Where are you from?" the guard barked.

"We are from the Colorado Territory," Case said. "We are not your enemy."

The guard's face eased. "You said your name was Case Tappan?"

"Yes sir," Case said. "You've heard of me?"

"Of course," the guard replied. "Everyone's heard of you."

"I need to speak to your sergeant urgently," Case repeated. "The United States is aware of your present location and is about to strike from above. You need to get your troops out of here immediately."

The guard hesitated and then removed his weapon from Case's back. "Turn around," he said.

Case and Renna turned and faced the soldier. Case's body was soaked with rain, and the scent of sweat, and thick muck. emanated from his skin, and he wondered how much more he could physically handle.

Water dripped slowly from the brim of the guard's helmet. His face was wet and dirty. "I think I should believe you, but how do you know so much?" he asked, his weapon trained at Case's heart.

"It doesn't matter," Renna said. "Texas has lost the element of surprise, and President Everett has ordered a massive airstrike."

"But–" the soldier started.

"Do you want to die today, soldier?" Case asked.

"No," he answered, his voice quivered. "I've got a family."

"Then take us to your sergeant," Case demanded.

"Follow me," the guard said, and he lowered his weapon.

Case reached for Renna's hand and squeezed it tight. Renna squeezed back.

The soldier knew where he was. Case figured he'd probably walked this path many times as a scout. The soldier stepped over obstacles with ease and warned them of oncoming depressions in the ground. In his desire to warn Case and Renna of what lay ahead, the guard wasn't paying attention to his own footing and suddenly tripped in a deep depression, twisted around, and fell awkwardly. His leg buckled as he hit the ground. His bone made a cracking sound loud enough to echo against the damp pine trees.

"Jesus," the guard hollered, as he gripped his leg. He lifted his pant exposing a protruding bone. "Oh, Jesus Christ."

Case dropped to his knee and tried to ease the guard's pain. "I need to straighten your leg out," Case said. "Renna, can you help roll him over?"

Together they rolled the guard over. "Holy shit," the guard said. They stood behind him, reached under his arms, and pulled him upright. They dragged him a short distance to a tree and leaned him against it. The guard exhaled hot, heavy breaths and grunted in obvious pain.

Case knelt and started to examine the leg. Renna tapped him on the shoulder. "There's no time for this," she said to Case.

"Renna, I can't just—"

"We have to go," she said.

"What?" The soldier cried. "Please help me."

Case leaned in close, the name on his chest read "Ruiz." "I'm sorry, Ruiz," Case said. "How far to camp?"

"About a quarter-mile," Ruiz responded.

"That'll take too long to carry him all that way, Case," Renna said. "I know you want to, but there's no time." She tugged hard at his arm.

"You can't leave me," Ruiz called. "Don't leave me."

"Which direction?" Case asked.

"No," Ruiz said. "I'm not telling you. I will show you as you carry me back."

"We'll send someone," Renna said. "Right away."

"Please don't do this," Ruiz said. "It fucking hurts."

Case shrugged Renna away from his arms and leaned into Ruiz. "Saving you could cost you your life and the lives of your entire platoon. Do you want me to carry you or save everyone else's life? What do you choose?"

"What do I choose?" Ruiz asked. He squinted his eyes and his body trembled. He stuttered as he started to speak. "It-it-it's not my choice to make. Either you help me, or you don't. I can't walk on my own."

"I will help you," Case said, reaching out to him.

"Case," Renna said. "We can't."

Case ignored Renna. "Come on," he said to Ruiz and opened both his hands to him. "I can haul you across my shoulders."

"Case," Renna called again.

Ruiz rubbed his leg but looked directly into Case's eyes. The grimace on Ruiz's face faded into a soft look of understanding, his thoughts were distant, yet his brown eyes were focused. "You're gonna carry me?" he asked.

Case nodded.

Ruiz grimaced in pain but made no motion toward Case. "Forget it," he said. "Go on without me. It's only ten minutes if you hoof it."

Case found the canteen of water attached to Ruiz's uniform, unlatched it, and handed it to him. "Okay," Case said. "It was your choice after all."

Ruiz nodded. "Yeah," he said. "I guess it was."

Case rose to the glaring blue eyes of Renna. She looked at him and blinked in disbelief, her lips straight and taut.

"What?" Case asked.

Her lips parted into a smile. "Nothing," she said. "Let's go."

They arrived at the camp in no time. Texas soldiers milled about under canopies of army-green canvas tents with the determined motion of insects within a colony. There was the clinking of metal, the sound of heavy boots crunching on the ground, and the distinct sound of steel sliding on steel as weapons were loaded, checked, and rechecked. Some men moved about without words, some sat alone, some scoured maps, others whispered soft utterances of prayer, all in preparation for the announcement of their final directive.

One man noticed the arrival of Case and Renna. He raised his weapon, and Case raised his hands.

"My name is Case Tappan from the Colorado Territory, I have no weapons and cannot harm you," he said.

"Case Tappan," the soldier said, observing Case's face. "You're alive? We believed you were killed in Eads."

Every time Case heard about Eads his heart ached. He wanted more than anything to get back to see what had become of his home, but he knew his destiny was to die without ever seeing Eads again.

"I have news," Case said. "Your platoon is under imminent threat from the United States. I have no time to get into details. I need to see your sergeant right away."

The soldier furrowed his brow. "I need to pat you both down," he said.

Case lifted his arms and the soldier patted him down thoroughly. "You can trust me," Case said. "I need your help."

The soldier nodded as he patted Renna down. "Follow me," he said.

A dozen army-green canvas tents protected the units from the weather, one of which they were escorted to. As Case stood under the canvas, gentle rain started to patter the top with a consistent cadence. Water rolled off the edges in steady streaks creating small moats of mud along the tent's perimeter.

The soldier spoke to one of the men in command, "Sergeant Miller. These men urgently need to speak with you."

Sergeant Levi Miller turned and faced Case and Renna, limbs akimbo. His face was brushed in a thin layer of mud purposely placed there as a form of camouflage. His eyes were glossy and tired. Case sensed the raw emotion of war within his sad look. At his post were maps and a satellite phone. He glanced at the phone constantly. When it rang, he'd pick it up, wait for the go command, and order his troops to attack the border of the United States. His expression was impassive, his fatigues ragged and unkempt, but Case knew he'd dutifully execute the order.

"What is it?" he asked. His voice sounded dry and raspy.

The guard deferred to Case. "Sir," Case started. "My name is Case Tappan of the Colorado Territory. The United States is aware of your position and is prepared to strike from the air. You need to retreat immediately."

"Well now, son," he said to Case all while casting a disapproving glance at the young soldier. "I know who you are, but you can't command this brigade."

"Sir," Case argued. "If I may–"

"No, you may not," the sergeant barked. He moved in close enough for Case to smell his sweat. An ugly smile moved across the sergeant's face. "You probably haven't heard. This land belongs to Texas now."

Case looked at Renna. She shook her head and shrugged. "What do you mean?" Case asked.

"A treaty signed by President Russo and Callie Stanton finalized that deal," he said.

"What? How? She can't–" was all Case could manage.

Renna exhaled loudly, visibly upset. "With all due respect, sir," she said to the sergeant. "It doesn't matter who owns this land. You need to retreat, right now."

"Get out of my face," Levi Miller ordered. "I've got work to do."

She tugged Case's shoulder and urged him to leave with her

eyes. "Come on," she said to Case. "We did our job. We warned them."

The soldier moved out of the way and let Case and Renna by. As they left the protection of the tent, rain tapped on their heads.

Then Case heard the husky voice of Sergeant Miller call from behind him, "Wait," he called. "How do you know?"

Case spoke loudly so he could be heard over the rain. "I heard the order issued directly from President Everett himself."

The sergeant's stance suddenly straightened, and his demeanor changed to one of engagement. "President Everett?"

The sergeant's phone rang and he turned to pick it up. Case saw his eyes shut as he listened. "I understand," he said. "There's rapid movement within the US. You need me to contact Russo for direct instructions. I see."

The sergeant dialed up a signal and paced about the tent. "Pick up," he said. "Damn it, pick up." His foot tapped rapidly. "Damn it, you fucker. Pick up."

Case felt Renna's hand on his shoulder. "Let's leave," she urged.

An eerie silence overcame the land. From the east, in the general vicinity of Prison Bay One, there was the echo of a massive explosion. Case imagined prisoner Walls's body being torn apart, finally freed from the tightening ligaments of tyranny.

"Pick up, mother fucker! We're under attack," Sergeant Levi Miller yelled into the abyss. He slammed the phone to the ground. "Damn it."

"Retreat!" Sergeant Miller yelled. "All units take cover!"

Renna pulled Case even harder. "Case!" she called. "Case! Let's go!"

Above, the distinct din of a jet sounded from the east, but Case didn't move. His legs were rooted in the soil, firm in his resolve. The land under his feet was familiar. The souls of those before him turned to blood and entered his veins. He realized if liberty were to succeed, he had to die right here so his story would be cemented in history. This was how it was supposed to be. He looked at his palms. They were dirty except for his fortune lines. They were clear of any mud. Case knew what he had to do.

"No," Case said. "You go."

Renna's face was that of bewilderment and confusion. "Case. You don't have to do this."

"You're ready, Renna," Case said, and squeezed her hand. "to pick up where I've left off."

"Case," Renna said, as tears formed.

Case smiled. "It's time to show the images of war and the reality of Everett's disturbed mind. It's time to show the world."

14

C allie sat on a soft armchair in the guest room of the Capitol Building holding a glass of red wine. She took a sip and allowed the smooth liquid to coat her tongue as she absorbed its fruity flavor. Across the room was the welcoming comfort of a king-size bed. Its beautiful white sheets and fluffy down pillows beckoned her. She closed her eyes and tried to relax, but her mind was too busy going over everything that had happened today.

Evening settled in and the soft light of the reading lamp offered a contemplative glow. As her thoughts steeped like hot tea, the shuffle of feet in the hallway outside pulled her back to reality. The shuffle stopped at her door, and shadows of shoes obstructed the light in the door's gap.

Whoever it was, lingered there. For a moment, Callie forgot about the recent weeks of her life. She felt as if this was her house, her room, and the person at the door was as familiar as a husband. She experienced tingling in her veins, a sensation of desire for something she had yet to experience with the person she longed to be with.

She rose and walked to the door. She rested her hand on the wood frame and waited for him to knock. She wondered if he could sense her presence on the other side; feeling each other through the invisible fibers of a wooden door. Her stomach flipped and there was a tension between her legs. She moved her hand to the brass knob, just waiting for him to knock. After a moment, she heard the soft shuffle receding from her room and going back down the hall.

Her heart beat in the pit of her stomach at his departure. When all was silent, she turned the knob and peered out. Aside from the pictures of oil rigs along the walls, the wide hall was empty. At the far end of the hall, she caught a glimpse of a door slowly shutting, swallowing the light from within. As far as she knew, only her brother and Duane Russo were staying the night. It had to be Russo. She pictured herself desperately racing to the door to find out why he hadn't knocked, but she refused to appear as desperate as that.

She closed the bedroom door and went into the large bathroom. She flicked on the light and it filled the room with warmth. She caught her reflection in the mirror over the marble washbasin. She expected to see a different version of herself, one that had aged and withered; hair that was frayed and broken, eyes that sucked into their sockets for fear of seeing any more of the horrors they had witnessed. Instead, her skin remained smooth, her hair was long and flowing, and her eyes were filled with brightness and life. She turned her head and examined her profile. She smiled at her reflection and spun around with youthful exuberance.

A bathrobe hung behind the white bathroom door. She disrobed, checked out her fit appearance in the mirror and slid the terrycloth robe over her naked body. Across the room was a deep, jetted tub adorned with candles and luxurious towels. She sauntered to the tub and closed the drain. She twisted the faucet handle marked with a red cursive letter H and ran the water until it was almost too hot to touch. She lit two candles with some nearby matches and poured bubble solution into the tub. The smell of lavender from the candles draped the air with a relaxing aroma. The running faucet sounded like a waterfall as it filled the tub. She walked back to the mirror and spun around. Her robe was partially open, exposing the top of her breasts. The flowing garment revealed a slender portion of her long right leg. All of her attractive body was the loss of the silent caller who wouldn't knock on her door.

She left the bathroom to pour another glass of wine and decided to take the rest of the bottle with her. She walked back to the tub, rested the bottle between two candles, disrobed, and sunk into the bubble bath. Warm water covered her skin like a liquid blanket. She closed her eyes and her stress lifted, yet a curiosity about the man behind the door persisted. Before she knew it, she had consumed the entire glass of wine. She poured another and allowed the alcohol to carry her mind adrift. She thought of Russo and his strikingly handsome looks. She poured another glass.

When the water felt tepid and her fingers wrinkled, she got up, drained the water, toweled off, and tied the bathrobe over her damp body. As she stepped out of the bathroom, she noticed the shadow had returned to the door's gap. Only this time, he knocked. The sound was soft but rapid, an anxious type of knock but not meant to alarm. It was a subtle, I-hate-to-bother-you type of knock. She let it happen again, just to be certain it was meant for her. The second knock was slightly louder, in case she hadn't heard the first one. She knew that would be the final attempt.

She pulled the drawstring across her robe, tightening it securely to her waist, and cracked the door. She first noticed his eyes, wide and amber-hued. It was Russo. When he saw her, his lips crested into a pleasant smile. It was the same smile he gave from across the table after signing their agreement.

She pushed the door open all the way, suddenly feeling self-conscious.

"Callie," Russo said delicately. He had not used her last name, suggesting the informal nature of his visit. "May I come in?"

"Yes, of course," she said. Her voice was low and suggestive. He was a man who was not afraid to act on his feelings. He was a man who trusted his gut. He was a man who wasn't going to let an opportunity pass him by. He was the man she needed in her life.

She swung the door open and allowed him to enter. He wore casual jeans and a navy V-neck T-shirt. As he stepped into the room, his broad, muscular arm brushed her just slightly, almost, but not quite inadvertently. His body smelled like a recent shower. She smiled as she closed the door and turned to him, anxiously awaiting the reason for his visit.

"I wanted to let you know the troops will be in place in less than an hour. They will set up a mini command center and wait for my direct order to strike. I've thought about it, and I think the command should come from you."

Callie's muscles throughout her entire body stiffened, not with fear, but with power. He wanted her to know she was in charge of what happened next.

"We have an hour then?" She asked, curling her finger through her hair.

"Yes," Duane said.

Callie tightened her robe and flashed a smile. Duane examined her outfit and smiled back. "I am so sorry to catch you like this," he said, his deep, luxurious voice echoing off the walls and resonating in Callie's ears. Hearing his voice was the auditory equivalent of eating chocolate, and her heart raced.

"It's okay," she said and looked down at the ground. "I had just finished a bath when you knocked. Did you come by before?" she asked, looking up at him. "I thought I heard someone at the door."

For the first time, Duane looked nervous. "Well," he started and then sighed. "It was me. I just needed to confirm the status of the strike before I updated you."

"I do appreciate the opportunity to set this in motion," she said, hoping to urge him into admitting that he was into her. "But do you think the troops will act on my command?"

Duane's smile widened. Callie didn't think her heart could beat this fast. "You just have to tell me when you are ready," he said.

"Okay," she answered. She found a second glass and another bottle of wine. "How rude of me," she said. "Would you care for some wine?"

"Perhaps something a little harder," he said walking to the liquor cabinet. "I happen to know where they keep the whiskey." The cabinet opened with a subtle squeak and inside was a bottle of aged whiskey. He poured two glasses. The amber color of the whiskey matched that of his eyes. He handed a glass to Callie.

She knew he wanted to stay, and she accepted the whiskey. Russo raised his glass and Callie followed. It was silent for a moment as Duane searched for words, but it was Callie who found them first. "To victory," she offered.

"Indeed," Duane said. "To victory." Their glasses clinked, and Callie drank the whiskey in one gulp. Intense heat from the whiskey coated the back of her throat, but she behaved as if nothing happened at all.

Duane shot his whiskey and poured them both some more. "I've never met someone quite like you," he said.

"What do you mean?"

"So direct and so passionate. You know what you want, don't you?"

Callie sipped her whiskey. The effect of the shot was already enhancing the buzz she had from her wine. Her body was loose, and her mind wandered away from the sober places it resided in the past four years in Colorado. She was on vacation and she was ready to let her drunkenness control her behavior.

"I am passionate," she said. She watched as he finished his

whiskey and poured another. "And I'm ready for this."

Duane furrowed his brow. "Ready for what?"

"Ready for whatever comes next," she said. She rested her whiskey on the end table. Her bare leg slid out from the bathrobe and she did not move to cover it up.

Duane blinked. Callie could sense his frustration. She could tell he interpreted her signs but wasn't certain if he should act.

"Are you nervous?" she asked with a gentle laugh.

"Me?" he responded with an airy voice. "No. Of course not."

Callie glanced at the clock on the wall, it ticked another minute away. She rose and walked toward the bed. "We've got forty minutes before our lives will forever change."

"What should we do?" Russo asked.

"Whatever you'd like," she answered. She reached out, touched his chest, and gently nudged him backward toward the bed. He stumbled just a bit but recovered easily. He held her hand to his chest and engaged her with his eyes. With her free hand, she touched his right arm. He flexed just enough for her to understand only a small potential of his force.

She stood on her tiptoes and ran her fingers through his hair. He kept his eyes on her, but his hand moved to the small of her back. They pulled each other close, and as they kissed, she felt her body tense up completely as his lips opened and closed, his tongue reaching for hers. She experienced the taste of his tongue for only a brief moment and then playfully pulled away. She felt his hands move up her spine toward her neck. Her robe opened just enough to expose her left breast. She reached over and covered it; he hadn't yet earned her treasure, though the smile on his face said he had managed to sneak a peek.

He placed his hand behind her head and drew her in. He pressed his lips hard against hers and they kissed again. This time she did not pull away. She moved her hands down his back and up the side of his thighs. Locked in their kiss, she blindly slid her hands toward the front of his jeans and grabbed hold of his belt buckle. She unlocked the buckle, slowly slid his belt off and wrapped it coyly around his back. She held the belt tight against his skin, pulled away from the kiss and pushed him toward the bed.

Duane sat on the edge of the bed. Callie snapped his belt away from his back and folded it. Duane's phone chimed loudly from within his pocket. Everything stopped. She glanced down, beyond the bulge in his pants at the annoying sound emanating from his pocket. His look was one of mortified disbelief. He reached into his pocket and tossed the phone aside without so much as looking at who the caller was. It bounced off the corner of the bed and landed with a clunk on the wood floor.

Without saying a word, he reached for her again and slid his hands inside her robe and caressed either side of her waist. His hands warmed her skin and she melted into his touch. She reached under his shirt and felt the muscles of his chest in the palms of her hands. It was as if her hands were meant to be there, completing a missing piece of a puzzle. He arched his back, inviting the removal of his shirt. She lifted it off his body and cast it aside.

His hands slid up her torso and cupped her breasts, he paused there for only a moment. Then he moved his hands over the top of her breasts, and she could not help but offer an audible sigh of satisfaction.

From the floor, the phone sounded again, disrupting the symphony of movement they were engaged in. The screen lit up with an unnatural glow, extinguishing the serene light of the mood.

"Damn it. Who keeps calling? Maybe it's important." Russo said. His breathy voice was evidence of the exhilaration of the moment.

Callie's body convulsed with excitement and impatience. "Let it go," she said and popped open the top button on his pants. He barely glanced at the phone as the voicemail signal chimed and the backlight of the screen faded into the dimness of the room, silent once again.

Her robe slipped off her body to the ground, like a perfect layer of whipped topping on the floor. He leaned back on the bed and looked at all her natural splendor and beauty. She smiled at his boyish grin with the wisdom of a woman. She moved toward him slowly, the soles of her feet sinking into the cushy throw rug underneath her toes. She kneeled to one knee and glided her hands up the inside of his thighs and unzipped his pants. As he lifted his hips, she deftly slid them off and threw them on the ground. She rose and fell into his arms. She allowed a moment to imbibe in the warmth of his skin on hers. Then he kissed her passionately. Callie's body focused on pleasure, but her mind wandered briefly into the future. Together, she and Russo were as powerful as any couple could ever be.

As his thickness entered her, years of desires denied reached a stunning crescendo of pleasure. Her entire body tightened and relaxed over and over and over again. She only noticed for the briefest of seconds the sound of Russo's phone ringing once again.

15

Case stood rooted in his native soil. The sound of jets fading in and out of range toyed with his ears, but he knew they were on their way. "I have to do this," Case said to Renna, observing the desperation and fear on her face. He reached out and held her hand. "Because you freed me, you did your part in freeing us all. Now it's my turn." He released her hand.

"There's got to be a different way," Renna said.

The last of the raindrops fell, and the gray, saturated clouds collectively huffed away like a slow-moving barge. Case fell to his knees and carved the symbol of the Colorado Territory into the soil. The wet ground allowed him to dig deep lines into the earth with his hands.

"This represents more than my life. This is how I show the world the images of war— the bodies, the gore, and the reality of Everett's destructive behavior, and this is exactly what I am supposed to do. Renna, you need to get out of here. You are the next voice. I trust you. This moment right here is now the story that needs to be told. And you are its author."

Renna sobbed. "Case," she said as she leaned in for a final hug. "I choose to tell your story."

Renna gently kissed his lips for the first time, and Case knew this tiring journey home was nearing completion. There was a longing in his soul as if he could see his porch lights waiting for him. Renna took his wet hands and squeezed them tight. As she let go, her lips were straight, but her eyes smiled. She then turned and ran for her life.

The fog lifted from the valley and the trees waved in a gentle breeze. Men scurried about frantically, some on phones, some hunkering in bunkers, some loading munitions. From above, three jets appeared low on the eastern horizon. Case's body quivered, but he remained rooted to this spot on the earth; his epitaph was imprinted into the land beneath him.

The distinct din of the jets quickly turned into a booming sound that tore at Case's ears. Within seconds they were overhead. From chambers in the jets' bellies, bombs fell. There was an eerie silence followed by the white-hot light of an explosion. Case buried his head in his hands and instinctively dropped to his stomach. The earth shook as the bombs gashed through the terrain with ease. Fragments of rock and men's bodies fell from the sky like a macabre hailstorm. Hard chunks of earth landed on his back. The pain was instant and intense. Something struck his head and he felt warm blood flowing from his skull.

The sound of soldiers screaming resonated in Case's ears. He may well have been inside a torture chamber. When the dust settled, he looked up. Desperate troops ran everywhere, their mouths in motion with silent screams. Sergeant Levi Miller stumbled into the open, blood spurting from his severed arm. He stopped and looked up at the sky. Someone came to his aide. He mouthed something before he collapsed.

There was another wave of loud jets from above, followed by the heavy thuds of helicopter blades slashing through the air. It sounded like hundreds of them, swarming like bees. Case tried to look, but the blades kicked up dirt and spat it at his face. The smell of gasoline and smoke filled his nose and all Case could do was bury his head in the ground. The United States unleashed weapons from the safety of the air, and only God could stop them now.

There was a lull the bombing; perhaps it was over. Case opened his eyes. Bodies lay strewn about; some intact and some not. Some were motionless, while others were taking their final breaths. Case put his hands into the mud and pushed himself up but collapsed when searing pain from the wound in his head hit him. As his blood contacted the soil and mixed with the blood of his ancestors, he slipped into a semi-conscious state.

His dreamy mind filled with the disembodied visions of those who had paid the ultimate sacrifice for justice. Of those who yearned for the quiet innocence of living life within its natural boundaries.

The pattern of a single glowing line with a white tail emerged. It swooshed about and formed the outline of interlocking prisms which subsequently broke apart to form cubes, and then bent to create spheres. The line moved with the simplicity of singularity; and while it could never redefine the shape of a circle, it could influence its rotation and direction. From somewhere in a past life, the spiritual howl of a lone wolf called to him. Its universal cry of freedom seemed to emanate from the nakedness of a new moon, bookending all of the global biomes with balanced precision.

The images and reverberations danced together in his head forming words, spoken like a soliloquy within. These were the words of great people who presented themselves in plain sight. It was in this moment Case realized they were never dead. And their motives and beliefs could never be accurately portrayed in a history book. The words were a creed passed down to select individuals cut from the same cloth—distant relatives connected by the DNA of enlightenment—each with a singular step to take toward the advancement of their cause. All along he'd been following a chosen path, and his role was to cut the tangle of brush in front of him, so the next person could see more clearly. He saw the smiling faces of those who had suffered the same fate as him. He now understood that the reclamation could take land but could never take their souls. In as much as these spirits surrounded his body, Case knew the essence of the Colorado Territory had always existed and always would.

The lines shifted again in his mind and formed an ancient image of a symbol that had always been. It was the same one he carved into the ground before the bombs fell. It was the same one drawn on the flag of the Colorado Territory. It was the same one created by his ancestors long ago, and it was the same one that will always exist as a beacon of freedom so long as there are people on the planet.

In the far-away distance in his mind, he heard a voice. It was a woman singing his name. The sound was divine and inviting and soon became the only thing he could hear. He was drawn to her but wasn't able to move to her. As her song grew louder, the voice became familiar. She'd been expecting him all along.

The voice lingered, but then stopped. Case found himself lost in the silence between life and death. His sensation was that of longing; longing for something he had yet to experience with the person he desired to be with. He wondered if she could sense his presence on the other side. His stomach flipped with excitement. He was about to pass.

Case's mind wandered and wondered, lying in the weighted suspension of the physical world when the voice returned. This time she revealed herself. "It's me," she said. "Renna."

Case's heart filled with joy. He'd known it was her all along, and he wanted her more than ever. Her hands wrapped around the back of his head. Her tender touch lifted him gently toward her voice. "Case," she said. Her voice was hurried and excited.

Her touch was warm as she held him tight and he felt the

heat of her breath near his mouth. "Case," she said again. Her voice sounded so natural and soft. He tried to remember a time when he had ever felt as passionate about anyone as he did now.

He felt her hands unbutton his shirt and touch his chest. Her hands pressed hard against his body. "Case," she said. "I want you to know that I love you. I want you to feel that love right now. Can you feel it?"

He did. Her hands tilted his head back as she pressed her lips on his mouth. As their mouths parted, he felt his chest rise up and down, each breath heavier than the last. Her caress was so powerful, so strong, so passionate. He felt his body transformed into waves—cresting, crashing, and ebbing.

"Case," she said, wrapping her hands around his face. "Do you feel that? I think you do. Can you feel me?"

Yes. He did. He tried to reach for her but could not feel his arms. He tried to kiss her lips, but only met air. He tried to open his eyes but couldn't. He could only sense her pressure on his body, and the energy in her voice.

"Can you feel me?" he tried to scream. "I can hear you. Can you feel my love?"

"Case," she said. "If you can hear me. Just know I love you. We love you. So many people love you."

He felt her mouth on his again. When she stopped, he felt her hands on his chest. "One...two...three...four...five..."

He heard more sounds. Loud sounds, like helicopters. He felt her lips. He felt her breath. He felt his lungs. He felt her hands on his chest.

"One...two...three...four...five..."

"Case," her voice was frantic. "Case. Damn it. Case!"

Then silence. Her voice was gone. Just as quickly as it had come. There was a moment of complete love. A sensation of peace overtook him. It was the peace he had always wanted. It was the peace he had always imagined to be real. The peace that was divinely etched into the symbol on which his body lay. If the world could only understand this, there would be no reclamation, for there would be nothing that needed to be reclaimed. If the world could only understand this, there would be no evil, because evil could not breathe in the pure oxygen of peace. If the world could only feel this, there would be no flags, because there would be no land in which any group would occupy. If the world could only understand, they would all choose to lie down on the muddy earth and feel the things he felt, absorb the things he absorbed. Soon enough, they would.

16

Callie lay in bed, opened her eyes, and stared at Russo's handsome face. Her hand stroked the creases in his biceps. The scent of their sweat lingered in the room like a sensual perfume. Her stomach was calm, and her heart was beating with a slow and steady cadence. It was a feeling of safety and being in his arms meant he would protect her from the brutality of the world outside.

As she lay with him, Callie wished she could project this feeling of security to the rest of the citizens of Texas, so they could all dwell together within a metallic canopy of peace. Freedom is the ability of its citizens to perform daily tasks in whatever way they choose without fear of the inherent evil found within the minds of fellow human beings. A strong military was the cornerstone of protection from the unknown, and she was ready to order troops into battle. The moment was nearing, and when it was done, Texas would be protected from the intolerant ideology of the United States.

Russo rolled over. He met her with a warm smile and the fire in his amber eyes said all that was needed. He lifted his body out of the bed and draped a sheet across his nakedness. She offered a demure smile and he responded with a quiet laugh.

He let the sheet drop playfully, retrieved his underwear from the floor and slid them on. Then he reached for his phone and looked at its face. Callie could see a small light blinking rapidly, anxiously waiting for voicemails to be retrieved. He nodded at Callie. As he retreated to the bathroom, she knew it was almost time to get down to business.

Silence fell across the room as Russo shut the bathroom door. Callie slowly moved her legs over the side of the bed. The air in the room was cool compared to the warmth of the sheets. She searched for her robe and found it strewn across the floor near the bed. She slipped it on and was instantly warmed. The room felt dark and Callie wanted to see the daylight. She walked to the window and peeled the drapes back. She was met not by bright light, but by gun-metal gray clouds which slid across the sky and covered the sun like a dreary old blanket. She pushed the window open and allowed the cool, moist air into the room. The scent of rain filled the space with its familiar fragrance. Callie yawned, shut the window, and sunk into the warm comfortable chair in front of the television.

She found the remote control tucked in the chair cushion and flipped on the television while she waited for Russo to return. The TV chirped to life. The simplicity of turning the television on from a couch reminded her of how hard it was to live without, yet how easy it was to return to such a luxury. A smile crossed her face as she sank deeper into the soft chair.

The television screen blinked unfocused pixels as it retrieved its satellite connection. It appeared to be tuned to some kind of war movie. The scene was that of a war-torn country. Callie was not interested in watching it. Something less intense would allow her to take her mind off of things for the moment. She changed the channel, but the same movie was playing. It was then she realized she was not watching a movie, but live news coverage.

She sat upright, raised the volume, and listened. "Again, you are watching breaking coverage of an airstrike initiated by the United States against Texas troops located in the Colorado Territory," the female reporter said.

The camera panned across a gruesome scene. Several bodies were lying on the ground motionless. "Jesus," Callie murmured as she stared intently at the television.

"This is obviously raw footage," the reporter said. She sounded sharp and harsh, completely stunned by the carnage. "You may want to take your children away from the TV."

The camera focused on two bodies, one lying on the ground and the other atop of it. As the camera zoomed in, it became obvious to Callie someone was performing CPR on a fallen soldier.

"There appears to be an attempt to save a life happening right now," the reporter said. "My God."

"We need to cut the scene," a voice from the TV studio called from some off-scene location.

"Leave it," the reporter snapped. "People need to see this."

Something caught Callie's eye. There was a familiar outline on the ground next to the body of the fallen soldier.

"This is just remarkable," the reporter said. "You are watching live coverage of an invasion of the Colorado Territory by the United States of America. We are now hearing the strike was against a Texas brigade located in the southeastern border of Colorado. You are watching an attempt to save the life of a soldier who has fallen on some kind of symbol carved in the ground beneath him."

Callie knew the person was lying within the symbol of the Colorado Territory. Her body tensed and she nibbled at her lower lip. The person performing CPR gave breath and then pumped the chest. The rescuer shifted position, revealing the face of the injured soldier. She fell to the floor, her robe flung open, and her jaw hung wide. It was Case.

"Case. Why?" she cried. Inside, she knew exactly why he was there—to stop this war.

Callie remained glued to the television as the rescuer worked Case's body. The sensation of pins crept over her skin and nothing else seemed to matter. "Russo," she said softly at first, her voice filled with uncertainty.

"Russo," she called out to him louder. She needed immediate comfort. Someone to tell her everything was going to be okay, but he didn't answer.

The news remained locked on the scene, and Callie noticed it was a girl who pumped Case's chest. She worked frantically yet rhythmically. The girl lifted her head and looked up as if she knew exactly where the camera was. The intensity of her youthful blue eyes beamed through the room like a laser and directly into Callie's heart. Her eyes were wet with tears and there was a look of desperate concern in her face, which is reserved for a lover. She was beautiful, and despite the tragedy unfolding in front of her, Callie's stomach panged with jealousy. That should be her trying to save Case's life, not some beautiful young girl.

From the bathroom, Russo screamed. "Fuck! Retreat now!"

He stumbled out of the bathroom wearing only his boxer shorts. His cell phone was still brightly backlit. His face looked pale and his hands trembled. His eyes searched around the room, seemingly lost in helpless thought. He scrolled his phone then threw it down hard enough to crack the screen.

"Shit," he yelled. "I don't—"

"Russo," Callie said. "You need to see this."

Russo came toward the screen and he and Callie watched as if in the clutches of a horror film. As the light from the television illuminated the fear on their faces, they bore witness to the realities of war. On the screen, Case's body convulsed and then ceased all movement. The camera panned out, capturing the limp, disfigured corpses of Texas soldiers.

"What have I done?" Callie murmured. Tears poured freely down her face. "What have I done?"

"Callie," Russo said. "It is not your fault." He reached out to her and rubbed her shoulder. Suddenly his touch was weak and somehow dirty. Callie brushed his arm away.

"Callie—don't turn away from me," he said. "We will rebound from this act of inhumanity on our land." Callie let Russo's words linger for a moment. Their land. Texas was their land.

"What can we do?"

Russo shook his head. "We are too young in our independence to match the military prowess of the United States. The pure cowardice of Everett to strike with such force from the air is telling. We will not stand down. We will build our strength and our resolve, and then we will defend our land with the full power of our military." The tone in his voice was angry, but there was strength in his messaging. He was practiced at the use of tenor in order to convince.

Callie turned away from the television and looked at Russo. Even as her body shuddered in fear, her heart found favor with the assurance of Russo's safety.

There was a knock at the door, and Callie knew it was Aaron.

17

In his room, Aaron ended a call with his advisor and threw his phone to the ground. The screen cracked and tiny shards of glass spread across the floor like clear, hissing insects. He cast pillows off the couch and searched desperately for the remote control. He found it buried between the crevices of the loveseat and powered the television on. The news panned through an area devastated by bombs. Dead bodies of Texans were strewn about the land, bloodied and dismembered. The horrors of war were being broadcast across the globe like he'd never seen before. These were the bodies of boys who trusted his decision-making to keep them safe. These were once the voice of resistance. These were the boys of Amarillo and the People's Army.

He snapped the television off and sat back in his chair, his heart pounded in his chest and he could feel the slow tingle of despair emanating from within. He pounded on the arms of the chair and rubbed his hands through his hair. His stomach twisted in revulsion. At that moment he would have preferred if one of the bodies pictured on the television were his.

Aaron rose from the chair and walked to the window. The sun hung low in the sky, peeking out from behind gray clouds, glorious as ever. It offered no remorse, no sympathy, and no accountability for innocently rising and setting every day, ready to cast its light upon the ills of the world.

He searched his pocket for his cell phone and then remembered he'd thrown it. He moved to the nightstand and silently slid the drawer open. Despite all of the technological and scientific advancements that had been made, inside the drawer, he found the tools he needed to change the world—a blank notebook and a pen.

He opened the notebook to the first page. He clicked his pen rapidly as his mind swirled with the intensity of a storm. Four years ago, when the first bullets flew in Amarillo, he retreated to his home, wrote his friends, and discussed a second revolution. They took up arms against an oppressive government and won. From it, the Texas Territory was formed.

Thanks to him, Texas was again a sovereign union. They were free to worship God without feeling guilty. Free to protect themselves with arms. Free to debate political discourse. Free to pursue corporate enterprise. Free to pursue profit. Yet something was restraining them from being truly free. They were surrounded by some kind of invisible boundary. There was something unnatural that seemingly *allowed* their freedom, versus something that protected their natural, God-given freedoms.

These men— No, his men, lost their lives not protecting their natural freedom, but protecting the entity that allowed their freedom. That entity was the government. The purpose of Texas's government served only to restrict freedom, never to enable it.

"When did this change?" Aaron asked himself aloud. The final moments of daylight flickered in the window as the sun's last fingers stretched toward eternity. It carried with it the acts of war for the entire universe to see, to study, and learn from. All governments throughout time, no matter how benevolent the concept was, always bore out the same result.

"When will we change?"

Maybe this was how Callie had felt all along. It took a massacre and an act of war, but he finally understood why she never came home.

Aaron knew what he had to do. He flipped the pen in his hands and wrote a letter:

President Russo,

Over the course of the last several hours, my recommendation has led to the direct death of several members of the People's Army. They died because I presented you with information and the opportunity to expand our own power and privilege. Perhaps it has taken bloodshed, or perhaps it's been inside me all along, but I've come to the realization that this is not the way nature intended for us to be free.

True freedom exists when good people can reasonably expect to go about their lives as they see fit. A coalescence of people in the formation of a government serve only special interests, impose their will upon the lives of others, and enhance themselves at the expense of individuality.

I have concluded that I have been a victim of brainwashing as old as time itself. When Texas was part of the United States, I was told to place my life into the government's hands. When that government failed, I became the individual that the people rallied behind. Today I stood by and complacently agreed to order them to their deaths for the benefit of you and me, versus the people we purport to protect.

Mr. Russo, I submit to you that government is nothing more than a profit center that feeds off the wealth of society in order to sustain control of its people. I can no longer be a part of this or any administration.

This is my official resignation letter. May our glorious God have mercy on your soul.

Aaron Stanton

Aaron signed the letter. He reread his words until he could have recited them. Perhaps he was just reacting emotionally again. He needed someone to talk to about it. He couldn't talk to Russo, so the choice was obvious—Callie. His sister would listen.

He rose too quickly and felt dizzy. He put a hand on the nightstand to steady himself, then tucked the letter into his pocket and slowly walked to the door. Callie was just down the hall, yet each step he took was heavy, and each breath was labored. When he reached her room, he paused a moment, held the letter tightly in his hands, and knocked.

18

Callie motioned to Russo's mostly naked body for him to get dressed or hide. He scurried into the bathroom. There was another knock, this time faster and louder. Callie knew her every action from this moment forward would be rapid and anxious. Bullets had shattered everything she once believed, and bombs had torn apart everything she had protected. There seemed to be no end to this vicious cycle of violence. Why should there be? It was fueled by the brutal mind of President Everett, enhanced by unstoppable executive powers brought about by a system that failed to enforce its checks and balances year after year, after year.

Over these endless decades, both sides of the political spectrum allowed the president more and more authority to expeditiously advance their preferred political agenda, thus bypassing the intentionally lengthy and slow process of congressional debate.

Eventually, the office of the president was sought not by patriots with a love for their country, but by egregious egomaniacs seeking nothing more than power and fame. This left the people at the mercy of the president, not the president at the mercy of the people.

Callie paced the room, hoping Aaron would just go away. She glanced out the window. The sun had set and clouds circled the moon like vultures, threatening to destroy the remnants of humanity with powerful strikes of lightning.

The knock on the door persisted, and she could no longer avoid the inevitable. She slowly cracked the door open. Aaron's face was quaking with anxiety and his eyes were glossed over with fear. It was evident he came not with answers, but out of a desire for solace.

Callie opened the door completely and Aaron entered. "Callie," Aaron said. "Have you heard?"

Her guilt returned like the ninth life of a cat, and her body trembled with the knowledge that she was responsible for the severed limbs of maimed and deceased soldiers she had seen on the television. "I watched on television. This is my fault."

"It's not," he countered. "It's entirely mine."

"Aaron," Callie started, pausing when she noted a tear in his eye. "You couldn't have known."

"I should have thought this through. That's my fucking job, Callie," Aaron said. "It's my job to anticipate risks. I let my emotions get in the way. I wasn't thinking."

"You were thinking," Callie said in a soft voice. "You were thinking of Heather."

Aaron nodded. "I couldn't set that aside. Now it has cost the life of someone else's sister. It has cost the life of someone's brother, father, and son."

"Don't do this to yourself," Callie said, reaching for his shoulder.

"I've never been defeated, and I just…" He pulled a folded letter out of his pocket, opening it just enough to display the words written between the soft blue lines. "I've given this a lot of thought," he said. "I am going to resign."

"Aaron," Callie said. "You can't." She looked away in silence.

"I have to," Aaron insisted.

"Why now? You've literally fought to be here," Callie said. "We can do this. You even said God has a plan."

Callie looked back at Aaron and waited for him to make eye contact. He couldn't even look her in the face. When Aaron finally looked at her, she saw the agony of an older brother abandoning his baby sister.

"It's not your fault," Callie said, touching his shoulder. "There's honor in making everything okay. You can do this. We can do this together. Don't resign."

Aaron stuffed his letter back into his pocket. "You're right," he said with renewed hope. "I won't give up. I can fight for the men that survived this brutal attack. We can come back stronger."

Russo exited the bathroom, fully dressed, neat and tidy, yet carrying the lingering satisfaction of a man who had spent the afternoon in bed with a woman.

Aaron glanced at him and then his eyes returned to Callie, still naked under her robe.

"Russo?" Aaron said.

"I heard everything," he said. "We will build a stronger army."

"What are you doing here?" Aaron said.

"I was just—"

"Were you with my sister?"

Callie looked away.

"No," Russo said. His face turned bright red.

"I see," Aaron said. "Men were dying, and you were doing what exactly?"

"Aaron," Russo said. "I was here to inform her of the situation."

"Wouldn't you call me first?" Aaron asked.

"Aaron—"

Aaron waved him off, reached into his pocket and handed

him the letter. "You're right, Callie. God does have a plan for me," he said and opened the door. As he exited, he turned and faced them. "You better hope he has one for both of you."

Callie blinked back tears. "My big brother."

"I'm certain he'll return. Just give him time to heal from all this," Russo said, his voice calm and reassuring. "Will you meet me in an hour to review our options?" His voice was suddenly stern and down to business. Callie nodded and Russo left the room.

Callie walked past the window. Rain pounded on the ground, caught in gusts of loud, harsh wind. The scent of the powerful storm seeped through the windowpanes and filled the room with its damp odor.

She rummaged through her dresser drawers and pulled clothes on. As she dressed, the television beckoned her. Her mind returned to the final images she saw on TV of a young woman trying to save Case. She had to see what had happened next. She flipped on the television and held her breath. The area was completely covered with media vans and helicopters. The banner across the bottom read, *AN ACT OF WAR*. When the camera panned out, lights illuminated the symbol of the Colorado Territory carved into the ground, but Case and the girl were gone.

19

Case awoke to the sensation of a damp washcloth across his face. When the cloth contacted his cheek, it sounded like sandpaper rubbing against the significant beard growth on his face. He couldn't recall a time he had ever worn a beard. He reached up and felt the hair on his chin. It was soft, not prickly, and was at least four weeks of growth. Beneath him was the forgiving support of a bed. He opened his eyes.

His tall, slender bookcase was perched in the familiar corner of his living space in Eads. Every shelf was adorned with notebooks leaning against one another for support. Each one was filled with his ideas and working philosophies. To his right, maps of the eight former states now referred to as the Colorado Territory decorated his wall. Sunlight poured through an open window, and he could tell by the shadows on the wall it was late morning. A sense of familiarity reached his soul and brought about a smile. He was home.

"I like that smile," Renna said. Her voice was warm and rosy. She wore no makeup and dressed in casual blue jeans and a white, low-hanging blouse that exposed the curvature of her breasts when she leaned over to adjust his pillow.

"Are you comfortable?" she asked. Case nodded, leaned back into the soft pillows and looked around.

"Do you know where you are?" Renna asked.

"Of course," he said. "My bedroom."

"This is different," she said excitedly. "For weeks you've not been able to answer that question."

"Huh?"

There was a knock on his bedroom door and Renna opened it. "That's probably the doctor."

Dr. Wilkins appeared on the other side and made immediate, welcoming eye contact with Case. The doctor shut the door and came to stand over him. Dr. Wilkins reached down and took Case's hand. "You look great today," he said. His green eyes were calm and reassuring.

"I feel okay," Case replied.

"Today is different, Doctor," Renna said. "He knows where he is."

"What exactly is going on?" Case asked.

"Case," Dr. Wilkins said, "I am going to perform a few checks on you. Is that okay?"

Case exhaled and nodded as he tried to piece his life together. There was something that had happened in Eads. The doctor touched the back of his head. There was a dull pain where the doctor placed his hands.

"Does this hurt?" Dr. Wilkins asked.

"A little," Case said. "What happened to me?"

"Sorry," the doctor said. "You sustained an injury to your head."

"But you'll be okay," Renna said. She reached out and touched Case carefully. She smiled, and Case's pain eased.

Information and images flooded Case's mind. "Eads," Case said. "How can I be in Eads? Wasn't it devastated?"

The doctor raised his eyebrows and his cheeks quivered ever

so slightly. "Not everything," he replied. "Though we're lucky to be in Eads at all."

A warm breeze came through the window. Case sat upright without the support of the pillows and placed his feet on the floor. His focus blurred when he felt a sharp pain in his ribcage. He winced and reached for his chest. "What?" was all he managed.

"Your ribcage was broken when Renna was—"

"Not yet," Renna said, waving off the doctor.

"Case, you were injured during the ambush. The pain in your chest will subside with time," the doctor said.

Case looked for answers within. His mind took him to a wooded area on the border of the Colorado Territory. There was screaming, but the memory faded after that. He shook off the image and focused on only one thing. "I want to see it," Case said. "This is my home. I need to see Eads. I want to stand up."

"Can he walk?" Renna asked the doctor.

"He's been in bed for so long, it's probably best to have him move around," Dr. Wilkins said. "Case, please stand up slowly."

As Renna and the doctor held him under his arms, Case slowly rose off the bed. His legs wobbled and he wanted to sit back down, but he managed to stabilize himself. "My God," he said.

"You don't have to do this," Renna said. The concern in her voice made Case want to move even more.

"Yes, I do," he insisted. The sudden picture of a sterile white room filled his mind. He remembered a hot orange explosion and recalled the image of a man name Reed hitting the wall and morphing into a broken pile of bone and flesh. The memory faded. Beads of sweat formed on his brow.

"Case," Renna said. "Are you okay?"

"I don't know," Case said as he moved his right foot forward. He felt strong. He felt stable. "I can do it," he said. "Can you let me go?" The doctor and Renna removed their hands from his arms and Case clumsily managed to get to the door.

Outside, the sun warmed his body, and the summer air

smelled of the prairie he had always known. Something was different though; there was silence the likes of which he'd never heard before. Case slowly walked by living spaces expecting to see activity within, but the only movement was the invisible wind carrying the souls of the deceased through the open windows and doors.

"The survivors buried the dead," the doctor said bluntly, as he escorted them past the living spaces and pointed toward the valley. "There, beyond that fence, is a stone marking their lives."

The threesome followed a meandering path until they came to the fence. Case smelled the upturned earth as he approached the undulating mounds of raw dirt concealing a gruesome reality.

"I'd like to pay my respects," Case said as the three moved forward. "Alone please," Case said. Dr. Wilkins and Renna nodded and backed off, giving him some space.

Case placed his hands on the fence and paused as memories flooded his mind like a giant wave. He envisioned bombs falling from the sky, and Sergeant Miller screaming "Retreat!" He remembered something hitting his head, and he recalled a moment of comfort as the faces of those that passed before him made their presence known. It was the same feeling he had here, as he looked upon the fresh graves of his fallen brethren. But was the loss of life worth it? Was it he who led them? Or had they chosen freely? Maybe Everett was right, and Case had unwittingly ignored his own influence. Now those that had followed him were dead.

He stomped the ground and squeezed his fist into a tight ball. Had the people now buried here been strong in their last moments, or had they quivered in doubt?

"To those silenced voices," Case said, his lips trembling. "It was me. I bear responsibility for your deaths. I wanted to be among you. I was ready to die." Yet, he had survived for some reason; he just wasn't sure why. "God, take this burden from me. God, if you please."

A breeze of no particular origin and no particular destination blew across his face. A flock of birds rose from beyond the cemetery and caught a ride with the spontaneous gust. It was a moment slowed in time but full of simple forward motion. Case sensed the believers around him. The feeling didn't scare him. Indeed, it felt natural and right. Freedom always moves forward.

The sun cast a ray of light on a single, slender red stone protruding from the ground. The stone's shadow lay on the soil, marking the time in which everything changed. Etched upon it was the symbol of the Colorado Territory. No words or names were present. Case reached out and touched the marker gently with his fingertips. It was perfectly minimalistic, and he knew everyone here died with an understanding that the cause ran deeper than themselves. Their unique souls were now interwoven into the fabric of existence; and upon death, became a true representation of the individuality of the human spirit. Like the breeze that escorted him here, Case knew they would all move forward, even those buried in the soil. He lowered his head to honor their absence as he also acknowledged their presence.

Renna approached alone, reached out, and gently rubbed his arm. "I never thought I could truly understand what this place meant to you," she said. "Until now."

The sun peeked through intermittent clouds and the rays lingered on Case's skin, offering what reassuring warmth they could. As he stood in the soft golden glow, he recalled laying on his hands and knees and scraping that image of the Colorado Territory into the soft, wet ground at the border. "I think I remember everything now," Case said. "When I heard the bombers coming, I thought I was going to die."

"You don't remember everything, Case," Renna said. "You did die on that battleground. Your heart stopped. I resuscitated you."

More memories congregated in his mind—the sensation

of her lips on his mouth and her touch on his chest. "It felt delicate," he said softly.

Renna's eyes met his. "Delicate? There was nothing delicate about it. I broke your ribs."

"Not that," Case replied. "Dying. Dying is delicate. As violent as it was, I just slipped into your arms. It felt right. It felt peaceful. I felt like I was home."

"It's funny," Renna said. "When your heart started again, you took a deep breath, rose, and walked with me. Do you know what you said to me?"

Case shook his head.

"That you wanted to go home," Renna said. "So, I took you to Eads. You are home."

Case reached for her hand, "Maybe Heaven is actually earth and God wants us to figure out how to get to Heaven alive." he said. He looked at the stone with love, but his heart remained heavy. "I carved this image into the earth in hopes that maybe somebody would see it. That maybe somebody would remember. I guess I failed."

Renna's smile was as bright as the sun's rays. "Case," she said with a breezy tone to her voice. "Everybody saw it."

"What do you mean?"

"Do you recall telling me it was time to show the world what President Everett was doing?"

Case nodded. It was right before she joined him in the river headed toward the border. It was the same moment he believed he was falling in love with her.

"I asked you how we were going to do that. Do you remember your answer?"

Case inhaled and scratched his beard. "I believe I said it depended on you."

"Uh-huh," Renna said. "I don't think either of us understood exactly what that meant, but it happened. We did indeed show the world."

"How?" Case asked.

"Do you remember Everett telling us he was sending the news media and cameras so the world could see what kind of savages we were?" Renna said.

"Yes, I remember," Case replied.

"He sent them, alright. And they captured me performing CPR on you. The whole world saw you die and come back to life within your symbol." Her smile spread across her face. "Almost immediately people across the globe researched its meaning. Case, we showed the world."

The sunlight twinkled on the marker. It filled him with optimism he had never experienced before. It was an optimism more powerful than when he signed the original peace treaty with the United States four years ago. The movement did not die. It was more alive than ever, and it spread not with roots, but with the light.

"Case," Renna said, her voice was high pitched and her words, rapidly spoken. "There was utter disgust at what Everett did. Protesters stormed DC, waving your flag and wearing your symbol on their shirts. Not only did it stop any additional attacks, but Everett was also forced out of office. It turns out his unwarranted acts of war were never authorized nor even discussed by the House of Representatives. He was impeached and his entire cabinet was removed from office within thirty days."

"Then there is time to negotiate?" Case asked.

"Absolutely, "Renna said, "The new President of the United States has already insisted on it. We're to meet as soon as you're able."

Dr. Wilkins joined them at the marker. "Case," he said. "I think you should rest now."

"I will rest for the night," Case said. "But I am ready. How do we get to Washington?"

"I only have to place a call," Renna said.

"Then do that," Case said.

Renna furrowed her brow. He realized his tone was that of

a drill sergeant.

"I'm sorry," Case said. "I just understand how fast darkness can overcome the light. And we have to act while the time is right."

"Which is now," Renna said.

"Which is now," Case answered.

As they walked back, there was a motion near one of the living spaces. It was a child pacing around his house. Case made eye contact and recognized him immediately. It was Henry.

A woman walked around the space carrying a bag. It was Elizabeth. Though she was only twenty-five, she seemed to have aged considerably. Despite the horrors that most certainly resided in her mind, she stood straight and strong. She rested her hand on Henry's shoulder and allowed a smile to cross her face.

"Case," she said, "I am so happy to see you up and around." Her voice seemed cracked and dry, yet resilient.

"Elizabeth," Case responded. "It is a blessing that you are here." She nodded quietly as they exchanged a warm, muted embrace. Her arms shook and her chest heaved with emotion.

"I went to warn the others of the attack," she said. "That's when I heard him," Elizabeth said. "He'd hidden inside a chest in Heather's bedroom, sobbing. I took him and managed to escape."

"Heather, then?" Case asked.

"She didn't survive."

Case's heart sank. "My God."

Case kneeled and picked Henry's chin up with the tip of his pointer finger. "You'll be safe with Elizabeth."

"He doesn't say much," Elizabeth said. "He talks to me though. I will love him as my own."

Case mentally captured the image of Henry's sullen look and would use it to make himself a better person. "Someday, he'll take up his mother's cause." He hugged Elizabeth again and moved on.

They entered Case's living space and said goodbye to the doctor. "I'll check on you before you go," the doctor said as he shut the door behind him.

Renna sat down on the edge of his bed. The look on her face was that of pure exhaustion. Case could tell adrenaline was all she was running on. He sat down next to her.

"How long have I been here?" he asked.

"Two months," she said.

"I guess all I can say is thank you." He reached out and held her hand in his. She was pure. She was magic. He allowed himself to feel her energy surge throughout his entire body. He allowed his barriers to tumble as well as his resistance to romance. He loved Renna. It was she who breathed life into his deceased body. It was she who fractured his ribs while pumping his heart. Within the blood circulating in his heart was his commitment to the movement, and now she was just as much a part of him as the movement itself. Tears formed in the corners of his eyes. They weren't born of sadness. They were tears of hope.

"Case," Renna said. "I think it's best you rest. I can leave for a while."

Case shook his head. "I don't want you to leave."

Renna didn't say a word. When she smiled, he felt she understood what his tears were all about.

He slid his arm up her back and they embraced. She tightened her arms around his body until his fractured chest hurt, but it didn't matter, the healing power of her being overcame any pain he was feeling.

The embrace merged into a seamless kiss. As they collapsed into each other on the bed, his reservations dissolved completely.

"Are you sure?" she asked, breaking their kiss.

"About you?" Case asked.

Renna smiled.

"More than ever," Case said.

20

A lone in his living space, Case fingered the soft backs of the leather-bound notebooks on the bookshelf while Renna prepared for tomorrow's trip to Washington, DC. Over the course of four years within the Colorado Territory, he had developed, tested, and documented his ideas within these books.

He gently slid the first volume from the shelf. He held it as if it were thin glass as he slid his fingers across the silky surface. The smell of earthy leather filled his nose and it took him back to the day he opened it for the first time, full of blank pages waiting to be completed with eager ideas.

He looked at the first page. The words "Peaceful Secession" graced the top of the old paper. He ran his fingers down the page and read. These sentences described the visions of a young man clearing the path for the next person. Given the events of the past months, he was behind on his documentation. His thesis about negotiating with Everett had failed. In its place was something he never imagined possible.

He replaced the first book and thumbed the spines of his

diaries until he reached the year 2030. He pulled it out and flipped to a clean white page. He absently tapped the blue tip of his pen on the notebook. A playful breeze flipped through the room and rustled the maps hanging on the wall. The mapped land now seemed frozen in a time when borders and fences mattered. The boundaries known as the Colorado Territory bled together. He realized now that as long as someone carried the ember of freedom, they were no longer restrained to the boundaries outlined on an old map. Case placed his book aside and tore the maps off the wall. He ripped them apart and tossed them to the floor. The torn ribbons danced in the breeze.

He wrote in his book: "Theory: We are no longer restrained by the false lines of a map." The words felt jumbled with emotions, but he'd organize it all later. For now, he simply wrote and wrote and wrote.

When he happened to write the word "Democracy," his pen stumbled over the letters themselves. It dawned on him that democracy was always destined to cannibalize itself. He wrote: "Democracy is despotism whose philosophy is secretly weaponized behind the thinly veiled mask of equality for all and special privileges for none. There are indeed privileges, and they are reserved for those who breathe the air surrounding Washington, DC. For the rest, the breath of liberty is harvested from the lungs of its people, drowning them in the endless river of tyranny. The only feasible antidote is anarchy."

Case, the anarchist, wrote more.

When a knock came at the door, Case placed his pen down and fanned through the twenty pages or so of the handwritten thesis. The sun, though starting to fade, streamed through the window with its familiar rays. Case stood and walked to the door. He opened it slowly, expecting to see the doctor, but what he saw nearly caused his heart to stop for the second time. It was Callie.

She stood tall and slender, but when their eyes met for the first time in months, her rigid stance softened, suggesting comfort in the simple act of seeing Case alive again. She wore a fancy, navy blue business suit. Her white blouse opened just low enough to accentuate her breasts. Her body filled her skirt with sharp precision, and everything from her feet to her face was clean. She wore red lipstick and she highlighted her dark brown eyes with eyeliner. Case could not remember a time he had seen her with makeup. There had never been a need to wear any. His imagined life if he had been with her. He gripped the door handle tight, and his knuckles turned white. He had to let her in or else he'd just stand there forever imagining himself with her.

Callie smiled, perhaps sensing his inner angst. "Case," she said. She took a slow step into the room as if she did not know whether to shake his hand, embrace him in a hug, or to throw him onto the bed and smother him with her body.

He opened his arms and hugged her. Their history could not be ignored, and for whatever reason, she was here. Case reminded himself that she was lucky to even be alive. "Callie," he said. "I was not expecting you."

"I've come to get Henry," she said. "I heard he survived. I am going to take him to Texas."

Case nodded. Callie loved Henry. He knew Henry would be okay.

"I thought I'd visit you first. After all, you are the most popular person in the world right now."

"I don't think so."

"You are," she maintained. "You were viewed on live television by millions. Case, I cannot even begin to tell you what I thought as I watched you that day. I was completely stunned. You know, I don't even know why you were there, to begin with."

A lump appeared in Case's throat as he thought about the reason he was there. "I was there to warn you," he said. "I thought you may have been on the front line."

Callie looked at him. The look on her face suggested it was somehow both the answer she wanted to hear and the answer she had dreaded. She sighed deeply and circled the room for a moment, staring at the papers on the floor, but not questioning their presence.

"I wasn't there," she said. "I was—"

"Safely in Texas," Case said, finishing her sentence.

"I'm here to explain some things. You deserve to know." Callie's voice was soft, yet serious. The events of the past few months had changed them both eternally.

"Okay," he said, motioning for Callie to sit in the small wooden chair next to the bed.

She glanced around the room. "Thank you, but I'll stand," she said and crossed her arms. "I was here when the attack happened. I can't tell you how hard it is to be back."

Case nodded and stood quietly next to the window.

"Case, if you could have seen the empty looks in the eyes of the US soldiers as they awaited orders, it would have terrified you. When they opened fire, the emptiness in their eyes turned to glee. I never want to be that scared again. Never."

"Callie–" Case tried to interject, but Callie raised her hand to stop him. She only wanted to be heard right now.

"You weren't with me," she continued. "I watched my friends— No, our friends, get shot in the back. You weren't here. Just when I needed you the most, you weren't with me. God help me, Case, if I'd had a weapon, I would've used it. I would've preferred to die taking one of those bastards out."

"Callie," Case said.

"Just listen," she said. "You were on your way to the United States to discuss peace while everyone here was dying." Callie turned away for a moment and paced the room. When she turned back, she pointed a finger at him. "You and your goddamn peace talks. How'd that go?"

Case waited to see if it was a rhetorical question. Her pause was long enough to suggest it wasn't. "It didn't go well."

"Do you know how many people died?" Callie asked.

"A lot," Case said.

"Too many. One was too goddamn many. My sister is dead. I

was the one who was going to have to stop it, not you."

"I never intended this to happen."

"You never intend anything, do you? That's the problem. You don't care. You're not an anarchist, your apathy is selfish isolationism." Callie shot back. "I'm beginning to think this is all about you and always has been. What I did was take action. I risked everything to get to Texas after watching my sister die. I managed to convince them to send an army to protect us from further destruction, and what do I get? Nothing. Not even a thank you. You, on the other hand, are imprisoned and then nearly die. Yet somehow it is you who gets the hero's welcome. You didn't brave the battle like I did, because if you did, you would have picked up a weapon and used it."

Case hesitated but refused to acknowledge that possibility. "Maybe," he said, thinking of the stone he almost threw at Renna's head. "But what would that have accomplished, huh? It would have served to prove that man uses violence as a first resort. That's what it would have proved. Hate is the seed of tyranny. Acceptance of this notion makes you the isolationist, not I. There cannot be isolation when we understand how we are all connected."

"If you could have seen the look in the eyes of the US general here. If you could have heard the vile things come out of his mouth. If you could have heard his dark tenor, you would know, as I do, there is evil within every person. An evil and a hatred darker than you could possibly think. I promise you hatred did not start as a seed. It is a sickness we cannot overcome."

"It's not their heart, Callie," Case said. "They've been brainwashed."

"I saw their heart," Callie answered. "It's black and there was no room for light."

Case rose and looked at Callie's stern face. "Is this why you came?"

"No," she said with a sigh. "It's not." The tension in Callie's face eased, and she changed the subject. "These papers on the floor—These were your maps?"

"They were," Case said. He looked at the shreds and he fought the urge to put them back together. In doing so, he realized how much easier it is for the human mind to think in terms of boundaries. From confinement in cribs to the walls of our houses, to the lines of our county, to the markers of states, to the flags of our nations, boundaries are everywhere—each one stealing a little bit of liberty in exchange for safety. Case realized that as natural as freedom feels, it's almost impossible to conceptualize. By tearing them up, Case challenged himself to resist the inherent comfort of borders.

"Why are they torn?"

"You wouldn't understand," Case said sadly.

"Never mind. The President of the United States has publicly invited you to Washington DC, primarily to discuss a new peace arrangement between the US and the Colorado Territory."

"I believe this to be the situation," Case said, mirroring her tone.

"You should know this is not possible," Callie said.

"Why is that?" Case asked.

"The land no longer belongs to you. I signed an agreement with the Texas Territory, it belongs to them now. As such, you have no authority to represent these lands. I do," Callie answered.

Case shuffled the papers about the floor with his feet. The first cool breeze of an early evening settled on the arid plains and a quiet chill rose on his skin. Callie was right. He wasn't here when Eads was ripped to shreds by bullets. He wasn't here for the first dark night when the bodies stiffened and their blood congealed. They were families, never to hold each other again. They were children, never to giggle together while hiding behind the tall prairie grasses. They were philosophers, never to read or write again. They were the future of the Colorado Territory.

"It was never mine, to begin with," Case said. "I don't recognize your arrangement with Texas."

Callie furrowed her brow. "It doesn't matter what you recognize or not," Callie said bitterly. "It's reality. President Russo is committed to rebuilding his army and protecting this land."

"Then his movement is one of reclamation, and no different than that of Everett's," Case said. "You see that, don't you?"

"How dare you—" Callie started. She stopped when the door of the living space swung open.

Renna entered the room, her face bright, her lips parted in a wide smile, her blue eyes beaming with excitement. Case could almost feel the giddy thrill of adventure emanating from her. When Renna noticed Callie, her excitement disappeared like a ghost in the daylight. Her lips pressed together in a tight line, she gripped her hands into fists, and her gaze tore into Callie like a knife.

The two most important people of Case's life stood opposite each other, their stares locked in a matter of judgment. But there was no comparison. He walked to Renna and stood by her.

Renna smiled and stood tall. "It's time to go, Case," Renna said. "The president has arranged transportation and it will arrive within the hour."

Case's heart punched his chest from the inside. It was overrun with excitement and passionate love. His heart behaved this way every time Renna entered the room.

"Very well," Case said. "I am ready."

"If you sign a treaty with DC, Texas won't recognize it," Callie said, her voice betraying her growing unease. "This is our land now, and we will have it. So why don't you join us, Case? Who do you think is going to protect you? Do you think the Reclamation Movement is dead just because Everett is out? There are still millions of people in poverty. There are still lots of people in the United States who will turn their back on you the moment you sign. Why don't you join us? We will welcome you."

"I am not interested, Callie," Case said. He reached for Renna's hand and squeezed it tight; partly for courage, but mostly because he wanted her to know just how much he cared for her.

"What do you think is going to happen here?" Callie asked, her voice high pitched and pleading. "Who offers you a better choice? We have a common enemy in the United States, and we'll do better together. Come to Texas and work with us. I can get you any position you want."

"I don't want a position," Case said. "And I'm not interested in what you have to offer."

"This shouldn't be so difficult," Callie said, "You almost died in an attack, and everyone in Eads is dead. Why would you want to work with your enemy? Why?"

Case hesitated as he searched for an appropriate response. It was almost impossible, but it seemed to him the United States was more willing to compromise than Texas. "Because I can change them," he finally answered.

"You are either unbelievably naive or incredibly ignorant," Callie said.

Renna shifted and opened her mouth to object. Case waved his hand to stop her. "Why is that, Callie?" he asked.

"Because you have nothing to back up this treaty with. Texas does," Callie said.

"Weapons, right?" Case asked.

"Goddamn right. Weapons." Callie said, as her mouth twisted into a snarl. "I said it–weapons. Weapons so we can defend ourselves instead of getting rounded up and shot in the back."

"Callie," Case started. "What happened to you? Have you always felt this way?"

"It was always in here somewhere," Callie admitted, touching her chest. "I've never felt entirely secure with you."

The words were real, and they hurt. Case lowered his head and released his hand from Renna's. He knew the comment contained a double meaning. What was it about Callie? She had a way to challenge his emotional state of mind. "The need for security is born from fear," he said, looking directly into her eyes. "If I sign a treaty with Texas then I am a victim of fear. And I am no victim. I am an advocate for peace."

Callie chuckled, shook her head, and walked toward the door. She looked at Case for the final time. She flashed a courteous smile at Renna. "Very well," she said, as she opened the door. "Then you shall die twice."

Case held Callie's gaze. Her brown eyes seemed to flicker and there was grief knowing that he once loved her. "But I know now that I will not die alone." Case placed his arm around Renna's waist as Callie left.

21

Case looked out the window of the jet carrying him and Renna to Washington, DC. The landing gear deployed and a bout of turbulence shook the plane as it made its final approach. He sat back in his chair, closed his eyes, and gripped the armrest in one hand and Renna's hand in the other. He rehearsed prepared remarks in his head to take his mind off the bumpy descent. Earlier, he scheduled a short talk in front of a joint session of Congress, and during the four-hour flight, he had worked on his remarks.

The wheels touched down and he opened his eyes as the plane slowed to an easy taxi. It stopped on the tarmac and he noticed swarms of people gathered nearby.

"Who are they?" Case asked as Renna looked over his shoulder and out the window.

"Media," Renna answered.

"Why? Case asked.

"I told you," Renna said. "You're a big deal here."

Case's shoulders tensed up as his concern over his very

public persona grew. He was not accustomed to this, and he worried more and more that some would view his celebrity status as leadership. He had vowed to never let that happen, but he didn't want to lose the opportunity for millions of people to receive his message, either.

"This is how easily it happens," he said. "Demagoguery."

"It's true," Renna said. "But I know you, and you will find the right way to handle this."

Case and Renna exited the plane. It was early afternoon, and when the door opened a wave of humid air swooshed into the cabin. Guards moved mobile steps and aligned them with the plane's door. When Case stepped off the plane, the bright lights of cameras flashing blinded him as hordes of reporters called out his name. He turned, helped Renna down the stairs, and offered a small wave to the crowd.

Upon descending, security personnel escorted them across the tarmac toward a waiting limousine. Their driver stepped out of the vehicle and opened the rear door. Renna ducked her head and sat down, followed by Case. The car drove forward as the flash of cameras continued from behind.

"That all happened fast," Case said. "Off the plane and into a car."

"Just a short drive to the Capitol Building," the driver said.

The vehicle quickly made its way on the highway and into DC. The Washington Monument rose from the earth like a slender thorn stuck in the skin of liberty. As they got closer to the Capitol, large crowds appeared along the streets. Case heard cheers and chants arise from the gathering throng. He lowered his window and listened. They were calling his name.

Someone in the crowd closest to the limo recognized his face. "There," a voice called. "He's in there!"

Case rolled up the window and looked at Renna. "What is happening?" was all he could manage to utter, as his heart pattered faster.

"This is crazy," Renna said. "I heard you were popular, but I never imagined *this*."

As they drove, Case noticed people holding flags and wearing shirts emblazoned with the symbol of the Colorado Territory. The crowds called his name and people flooded the streets, impeding the forward progress of the limo. The driver stopped and honked the horn.

"What do we do?" Case asked.

"They want you, man," the driver said. "If we want to get to the Capitol, you need to acknowledge them." He pointed to the sunroof. "Why don't you wave or something?"

The driver slid the roof open. Case glanced at the square of blue sky, his ears filled with the sound of his name and his body shook with excitement. He looked to Renna for advice. "Should I?" he asked.

A smile spread across Renna's face. "This is your moment," she said. "Don't be scared. I think they are here to support you, not to worship you. Rise up and feed on their energy. The source of their vitality is the light inside of you. It gives us all courage."

"I can't let them down," Case said. "I won't let them down."

He rose and extended his head out the top of the limo. The roar of approval was deafening. Hands waved, women screamed, and men offered shouts of support. "We love you... You can do it... You are our only hope."

The weight of it all was heavy on Case's shoulders as he formed his fingers into a V. He knew there would never be an opportunity like this again and he had to deliver them to freedom. The limo slowly crept forward as the crowd parted. As he waved, a tear formed in his eye, like that of a new father witnessing the birth of his first-born child.

The limousine entered the gates of The Capitol Building. Case lowered himself into the car. Renna leaned in for a kiss and Case obliged. When their lips touched, electricity shot through his lips and directly into his heart. He opened his mouth and allowed the warmth of her breath into his soul.

"My God," Renna said. "I've never felt anything so good."

"Renna," Case said, his mind returning to the task at hand. He pulled the speech from his pocket. "You know the speech I wrote on the plane?"

Renna nodded. "Yes, of course."

He tore it in half. Renna gasped. "What are you doing?" she asked.

"I realize now what I have to do. I only ask that you trust me," Case said.

Renna's look of bewilderment gave way to one of acceptance. She sat back in her seat and relaxed. "Case," she said. "You pulled me free when I was left for dead. On the way to the border, you taught me valuable lessons. I defected from my own country and risked my life to free you from certain death. I resuscitated you on the battleground and cared for you afterward. I will always trust you."

She took Case's hand and rubbed his palm. He felt the worn roughness of war etched within both their fingertips. It reminded him that liberty was never to be taken for granted. Someone is always looking to take it away, for there is nothing more valuable than the fruit it produces.

The car slowed and stopped within the shadow of the Capitol Building. The driver got out and opened their door. Case and Renna exited and were escorted to a large anteroom. The tall, ornate walls were exquisitely decorated with art tucked into gilded frames. The art was a timeline of American history, and as Case's eyes moved from time period to time period, he noticed the Second Civil War was suspiciously absent. Perhaps it had been removed by the revisionist artists of American history known as Congress.

Case noticed a chill in the air. The ease in which he could be erased was likely as quick as his flirt with fame. The heavy door of the anteroom opened and the newly elected President of the United States, Randal Harper, emerged. He wore a navy suit and a red tie. A miniature flag of the United States was pinned perfectly to his lapel. Harper met Case with a handshake that was loose and amicable. When he smiled, heavy wrinkles lined his eyes. His white hair suggested someone experienced enough to have gained some wisdom, and the look on his face was inviting, honest, and ready to accept what Case had to offer. Case was reassured, but nonetheless, his stomach flopped at a nervous pace.

"Mr. Tappan," President Harper said. "It is a pleasure to finally meet you."

Case nodded. "Likewise," he said.

"I sure hope you are feeling better."

"I am. It was apparently a longer recovery than I was even aware of."

"Well, I must say in the months that have passed since you were resuscitated, the United States has changed. Our people are eternally grateful to you. If it weren't for your courage, God only knows what terror the Reclamation Movement would have wreaked."

Case lowered his gaze. "I do not wish to even ponder the notion," he said.

"Well, you needn't worry anymore. While not everyone is ready to negotiate, I assure you the majority of this Congress and I are willing to execute the will of the great people of the United States. And I am certain you noticed as you drove in today that the people have spoken."

"The crowds were rather humbling," Case said. "I owe it to them."

The president nodded and turned toward Renna. "As for you, Private Jensen, I have granted you full immunity. You are free from any prosecution as a result of your actions freeing Case."

"Thank you," Renna said.

"Mr. Tappan, there will be plenty more to discuss during the formal contract negotiation and signing ceremony. But for now, the Chamber is full and all the representatives of the United States are ready to hear what you have to say." The president rested his hand on Case's shoulder and gestured toward a door.

Case's palms were tacky with sweat, and he shifted his gaze from the door to the floor and back. He reached inside his pocket and remembered he had torn apart his prepared speech. Inside this room, he was with the one he loved and was about to speak with people who wanted to hear what he had to say. Outside the Capitol Building, he was surrounded by throngs of supporters, but at this moment he was very alone.

Case took a deep breath and said, "Let's go."

President Harper opened the door. The sound of speech within the Chamber bounced against the walls in a cacophony of simultaneous voices. As he entered the room, there was a hush that settled like a wave breaking against his feet.

Several lawmakers sat with mouths open in wonderment and curiosity. Case recognized those who were holdovers from the Reclamation Movement. They didn't want him here. The scowls on their faces were evident. Case may as well have stolen the keys of a treasure chest filled with gold that belonged to them.

Case navigated down a carpeted stretch of floor toward the familiar House podium. The one he'd seen many times during the State of the Union speeches. Renna found a seat in the front row of the chamber. Case and President Harper made their way up a small set of stairs. He stood beside Harper as he introduced Case to the representatives and senators.

"This is certainly a historic day," the president began. "I am so pleased to be here. Today is the first day of a new peace for our country." The room remained quiet as Case and the lawmakers listened.

"We have two special guests with us today. Neither of whom would be alive today if not for the other. Please welcome Case Tappan and Private Renna Jensen. As you all witnessed on live television, Private Jensen saved the life of Mr. Tappan, leading to a movement the likes of which we have never seen. A movement so powerful, a sitting president, the vice president, and the entire administration resigned under pressure from the people. This is indeed how our government was intended to work."

Case stole a glance at Renna. Her face was beautiful, and she beamed with pride. President Harper rambled on about the importance of peaceful negotiations with the Colorado Territory. But whatever he said no longer mattered. For the love of Renna and for the love of the Colorado Territory, the words he wanted to speak were flooding his brain faster than he could keep track of them. He was ready to deliver his speech.

"So," President Harper said, in conclusion. "Before we read through and sign the treaty, I'd like to invite Mr. Tappan to the podium to say a few words."

As Case rose and walked toward the podium, his heart beat faster and faster. It wasn't until he looked out over the crowd of blue suits, white shirts, red ties, and blank faces that he understood his heart beat not in anticipation of the speech but for his love of Renna. All he had to do was look into her eyes, and they would carry him away to a place only the two of them would know.

Case placed his hands on the podium. The lights in the room seemed brighter. He stood silently, taking it all in. President Harper raised an eyebrow, waiting for Case to recite his prepared speech. Case cleared his throat and began to speak.

"You have invited me here today to sign a treaty. One in which there will be peace between our two lands. It will likely be similar in nature to the one signed by us not long ago. And in only four short years, I found myself nearly dead within the boundaries of the land granted to me. I was fortunate enough to be resuscitated by an army private. And when she breathed into my mouth, she not only revived me, she revived the nearly extinguished flame of liberty. Moments like these are fleeting and tend to slip into the dark spaces of distant memories where they are entombed in the minds of the deceased and the dusty annals of history books. From time to time these books are brushed off and scoured; the thoughts therein are honored as interesting, but unsustainable. The ideas are relegated to the unenlightened who believe only a congregation of governance could know what is best and how to best deliver it, whether it is the economy, war, life, death, empathy, jealousy, or happiness. Government functions as the mind for the weak and meager who seek no alternatives because it is too difficult."

Case felt his nervousness evaporate. He leaned into the slim microphone. Harper's eyes shifted nervously.

"The United States has become a country of armed men with stale rhetoric not a country of visionaries. No longer has American thought evolved with global times. Instead, the US has opted to stagnate and swelter in the moldy pond of tradition and dissonance.

"I have made my way here today from a very far-away place, and I do not mean Eads, Colorado. I am talking about a place found only in the rational subconscious of your mind. It is within that subconscious where questions are formed. So today, I invite you to visit this far-away place and ask yourself this: What if there was a different way? What if the land belonged to no country? What if there was nothing owned by the government to protect? What if there was nothing owned by the government to control? What if you woke up every day and there was no government? What if the government didn't tell you what to do? What if the government didn't tell you how to think? What if there was no government to collect taxes? Better yet, what if there was no money at all? How would that look? Would we all fail to help each other? Would we all fail to deliver the things we need? Would we stop thinking? Would we not produce? Would we not dream? Would we not pray? Are we not people? Are we not the individuals of this world?"

Case looked around at the vastness of the utterly silent chamber.

"I submit to you that it would not end in the apocalypse as those who seek power will tell you. Fear is a tactic used first by the fallen angels and delivered to us by certain fruit trees. Spit out your rotten apple and partake of the pear. It is within these seeds that we can find ourselves again. When we do, my hope is we do not identify as a nation, nor as actors in a macabre play for the satisfaction of the kings who sit upon the velvet thrones of time, but for ourselves. Seek to cultivate the ground of your personal pear tree for it is from these seeds that we can provide for those who hunger for the ripest of pears and linger in its pleasant shade of ideas.

"What shall you seek in return, you ask? The answer is to seek absolutely nothing in return. And if some man lays claim to your tree and arrives with a chainsaw, you let him take the tree. And while he saws off his own legs and dies under the rot of his fallen tree, you will find there are plenty of others who will provide for you a sapling and a shovel.

"You see, we have a natural human desire to seek fulfillment and satisfaction in our lives. Would we, as people, not feel satisfaction working to cure disease even if there were no compensation? Would we, as people, not feel satisfaction producing food? Would we, as people, not feel satisfaction producing technology if it advances our lives? Would we, as people, not build homes for our children?

"In your heart, you know we would, because that's what we did in the Colorado Territory. We would focus on the things that matter and not on the things that waste our creativity for the sake of a dollar. It is the dollar that divides us. Paper money is the fertilizer of the seeds of jealousy. It is money and ownership of completely useless physical things that foster hatred and fear. Yet we have not evolved past its allure. It has caused our minds to fester and stymie the philosophic, moral, and ethical evolution of society."

Case opened his arms to the Congress. "We can do better. Before I came here, I was staring at the maps of the Colorado Territory on my wall. I ripped them off my wall and tore them to shreds. Today, I ask you to do the same. Tear up your conceptions, tear up your maps, tear up your documents, and tear up your treaty. I will not sign your treaty. Take what you think is yours, because someday, someone else will want it and take it. Take your land if you feel you are the rightful owner. Take the black profits of oil from the mountains of Colorado if you think it is yours, just know someone else will lay claim to it too. Take your territory if you must, but I will never sign away my life to you. My life belongs to me, and I will use it to make a better place for us all, regardless of where that place is."

The room was as quiet as a still-life painting. Case could almost hear the smile of approval creep across Renna's face.

After a moment, he walked away from the podium. Some lawmakers searched the ground, contemplating, while others rolled their eyes in disapproval, but they all waited for what was to come next. Case walked down the steps and over to Renna and offered her his hand. She took it tightly and rose from her seat. Together they walked out the door.

Outside the Capitol Building, Case and Renna were met with the loud murmurings of the gathered crowd. From their vantage point, they could see past the fence and into the streets. There were waves of people stretched back as far as the eye could see. Case and Renna stopped at the front gate. There was the briefest moment of utter silence before the crowd erupted into an explosive cheer as recognition of the two set in.

Directly overhead, the afternoon sun cast a warming light. Within the crowd, a man rose from a wheelchair wielding crutches. He wore a T-shirt with the symbol of the Colorado Territory. Case recognized his face. It was Ruiz, the Texas soldier who broke his leg while escorting Case back to camp, and who chose to suffer so Case could warn his friends of the impending attack.

Standing behind Ruiz, was Aaron Stanton, gripping the wheelchair from which Ruiz rose. Aaron smiled widely at Case. "Mr. Tappan," Ruiz called out.

"You made it out alive," Case said.

"I did," Ruiz said. "I am so thankful to you."

"No need to thank me," Case said. "I did nothing."

"That didn't take very long in there," Aaron said. "What have we got?"

Case placed his hand on Ruiz's shoulder. "My friends," he said, "you've got everything you ever needed and nothing you ever wanted—if you can keep it."

Case turned and reached for Renna's hand, warm with the ember of liberty. Together they melted into the crowd knowing that wherever life took them they would always be home.

About the Author

Jon's credo is that individuals naturally gravitate toward the positive energy in life, and are at their best when left to their own devices. For good or bad, his work will always explore this proposition. When not writing, you can find Jon at his Colorado based ranch introducing his two rambunctious boys to mother nature.